No Quarter!

Airship 27 Productions

Jezebel Johnston- No Quarter!
(Volume 10 of the Jezebel Johnston series)
© 2026 Nancy Hansen

Published by Airship 27 Productions
www.airship27.com
www.airship27hangar.com

Cover illustration © 2026 Michael Youngblood
Interior illustrations © 2026 Rob Davis

Editor: Ron Fortier
Associate Editor: Jonathan Sweet
Marketing and Promotions Manager: Michael Vance
Production Designer: Rob Davis

ISBN: 978-1-969285-07-3

Produced in the United States of America

10 9 8 7 6 5 4 3 2 1

Jezebel Johnston
No Quarter!

by Nancy Hansen

Other books in the series:

Jezebel Johnston: Devil's Handmaid
ISBN: 978-0692524039

Jezebel Johnston: Queen of Anarchy
ISBN: 978-1946183088

Jezebel Johnston: Sea Witch
ISBN: 978-1-946183-15-6

Jezebel Johnston: Mourning Star
ISBN: 978-1-946183-37-8

Jezebel Johnston: Birth of a Buccaneer
(collects volumes 1-4 in the series)
ISBN: 978-1-946183-49-1

Jezebel Johnston: Danseuse
ISBN: 978-1-946183-62-0

Jezebel Johnston: Sisters of Vengeance
ISBN: 978-1-946183-77-4

Jezebel Johnston: Mastiff
ISBN: 978-1-946183-98-9

Jezebel Johnston: Revelation
ISBN: 978-1-953589-13-2

Jezebel Johnston: Rise of a Buccaneer
(collects volumes 5-8 of the series)
ISBN: 978-1953589361

Jezebel Johnston: Captain Johnston
ISBN: 978-1953589651

Jezebel Johnston:
No Quarter!

PROLOGUE

Jacques Chagall had lived through many dangerous situations in his life, for he was a crusty old buccaneer with a streak of mean and some luck in his favor. He survived Henry Morgan's gunshot as well, for the ball had to penetrate both his leather coat and breeches to hit his sagging belly. With the small pistol Morgan carried being hastily drawn below the table, the shot was not carefully aimed, and it went somewhat sideways before it struck. The ball managed to miss any internal organs, though it nicked the hip bone just above the joint with the femur and then lodged under the skin where it was easy enough to be dug out. It bled quite a bit and was painful for weeks with a small and stubbornly spreading pocket of infection that spiked a fever. Chagall was laid up for some time with nothing to do but sleep in a laudanum haze or lay still and plot his revenge, but he did manage to get through it by buying himself a sickroom stay in the cramped attic of a local brothel owned by someone other than Morgan.

Chagall was also not a man who trusted anyone, not even those he had sailed with for years. When he had initially heard that Lucien Lévesque was going around to Caribbean ports recruiting anyone who owned ships or men serving with uninterested captains to join him on an extensive raid of the coastal colonies of the Spanish Main, wily old Jacques had secreted away some additional coin and small items from his East Indies take for himself. He had managed to lay aside enough to start over again with a new crew, for he expected to lose most of the current ones after they spent all their share of the cargo sale and were now listening carefully to what Lévesque's cohorts were telling them of the bountiful prizes their leader would potentially collect. So, it was no surprise when the majority of them sailed off with the now empty East Indies trade ship, leaving Jacques alone on *Danseuse* with just Arnaud and a couple other loyal men aboard. Once Morgan won that ship for himself in the draw of cards and shot Chagall when he called Henry a cheat and drew his own weapon, the old French pirate lost even those few men who were left, though *Danseuse*'s young quartermaster did come find him to let his former *capitaine* know he too was now looking for another berth.

Arnaud had found Chagall comatose from the laudanum and so asked the Madam of the brothel to write a note for him. She knew little French but Chagall could read English well enough.

I am sorry Mon Frère, but I cannot afford to wait ashore until you recover, though I am very happy to find you still amongst the living. I must sign aboard another ship, since Morgan tells me he now owns ours. That is, providing I can even locate a capitaine who needs me. I assure you it will not be with Lévesque! I hope to be back someday and find you well and ready to head out once more.

Arnaud.

Chagall was not a young man, so his recovery was slow. The wound had become infected down to the bone so would remain painful long after it had healed, and it left him with a permanent hitching limp. Yet it would be many months before he would be able to go back out to sea, and then simply as yet another aging freebooter aboard someone else's vessel. His money, so carefully hoarded, was now almost gone. He was bitterly angry with Henry Morgan for ruining his health, stealing his beautiful little ship, and taking away his livelihood after all those years on the account, and so swore an oath of vengeance on the smug Welshman.

This was how the Age of Buccaneers began to draw to a close, with younger, more ambitious as well as increasingly ruthless and dissolute pirates coming up through the ranks. The 'Brethren of the Coast' took on a new meaning as larger, increasingly audacious, and far more dangerous raids were planned. The Spanish Main became less lucrative for taking on the now well-guarded Flotilla and more so for bombarding or invading the wealthy colonies ashore with large parties. Some pirates banded together to attack the mule and donkey trains that hauled the output of mines overland. Others targeted similar caravans filled with the cargoes of Spanish trade ships coming back from the Orient, which often unladed on the Pacific coast of the narrow area above the great southern continent rather than precariously sailing all around it. The West Indies was producing far less lucrative prizes as it became more settled and better guarded. Slaves had become the most profitable incoming shipment to the Caribbean colonies, for increasing numbers of planters as well as the sizes of the plantations of sugar cane and spices were taking over their economies.

Some pirate eyes turned toward the scantly guarded eastern coast of the North American continent, which was becoming a hotbed of colonial acquisitions that the big European trade ships served regularly, bringing in manufactured goods to exchange for things like furs, lumber, tobacco, whale oil, baleen, and dried fish. While those northern waters were far colder and much of the coast forbidding, coming back with a full hold of cargo to sell at great profit to the more established Caribbean colonies made up for that. The pirates who raided up there became more bloodthirsty and barbaric cutthroats than their buccaneer forebears...

CHAPTER ONE

J ezebel Johnston left Antonia Campos' home early that evening, not even staying to sup with her distraught friend or her own family. For one thing, she had a ship to move up to the docks and unload the next day, the sound of which had perked up both the former Spanish hidalga and her own mother's low spirits. Antonia promised she would send Jobah and her helpers down to the docks with the wagons in the morning to take whatever cargo they had. They could inform the harbormaster that a ship was coming in to unload for Mistress Campos' shop. Things would go faster if they didn't have to tie up extra time at the docks explaining who they were and then waiting for some conveyance to show up.

She should get back to the ship soon, but first an angry Jez wanted to see if she could locate those two former crewmates who had threatened Antonia and Monifa as well as her younger siblings, and at the very least talk some sense into them.

Evening was the best time to find any seafarer whose ship was in port lingering about on dry land. It did not sound as if Sol and Jengo had been in Tortuga very long when they made their way up to Antonia's warehouse shop. Those two should still be out enjoying themselves somewhere.

She would hunt them down, and then Sol was going to get at least a piece of her mind, if not a taste of her swordsmanship. She was not above calling him out for what he had said to Antonia. It figured he would wind up signing with Lévesque, for Sol was always a shifty, sarcastic, and indifferent man, more of an idler and lickspittle rather than someone others would follow.

That Jengo had been with him when he threatened Antonia and her mother troubled Jez greatly. She was glad to hear he was still alive because she really liked the hulking, ebony-skinned former slave, who always had a big smile and something amusing to say. Why he took up with Sol, and had he also signed on with Lévesque, was something she needed to know, because unless Jengo had changed much in the intervening years, he was someone either she or Walter could use aboard ship. Jengo had always worked hard and as a fighter he was unsurpassed, yet he never lost himself in bloodlust with the innocent or those who laid down their arms and asked for mercy. This was a troubling change in him, that he would come well ashore to threaten two women.

She hunted down by the new docks and the buildings that housed the businesses that served them, asking if anyone had seen Captain Peter Solomon and his big negro companion. Some had seen them recently, but not so far this day. The question was, were they still somewhere on Tortuga or had they sailed off? It was pointed out to Jez that the old brig being refurbished out on the newly rebuilt dry dock area was Solomon's ship, so the captain and what passed for crew should be somewhere ashore.

Since they had enough money to remake an entire ship they were likely still in town, perhaps spending some of their coin in places where men tended to go when they were idle for a while.

Jez hit every tavern and rooming house that would rent to a pirate while looking for them, with no luck. She gritted her teeth in frustration because that meant she would have to check the brothels, something she dreaded. They were a part of her growing up years in Tortuga and an ugly potential end to her life in India; memories that she preferred to leave behind. She still felt sorrow for poor little Lía, the mixed Portuguese and African native girl who had been purchased by the same Arab slaver in Goa that Jez had been sold to. Lía had felt abandoned by both the culture and the religion she strove so hard to be part of, so in anguish had taken her own life rather than be sold into prostitution.

All of the brothels in Tortuga had been down in the harbor area and they had burned down after the Spanish bombardment. The small handful of replacements were now hidden behind the more legitimate businesses like taverns and suttlers, where they wouldn't offend the eyes of the fine folk disembarking from ships they had taken passage on. The strumpets themselves still strolled the nearby alleys and lanes, the boldest ones stepping out on the newly laid promenade looking for customers, though their manner of dress and language was far more subdued than it had ever been. In fact, it took a practiced eye to sort them out from the plantation wives, the female family members of the fisher folk, or trusted slave women sent down to shop in the marketplace. Much of the public bawdiness and catcalling, the scanty clothing and open propositioning was gone, with any assignations made outside the brothels agreed to in quiet terms.

Tortuga had been far wilder and more open about exposing its immoral underbelly when Jez was growing up, and yet she had roamed the dirt packed streets and alleys like any other barefoot harbor urchin, savvy enough to avoid anything that seemed dangerous. That was another reason she took so well to pirate life, for by the time she was old enough to toddle after the bigger children, she had seen her share of fights, deaths, drunkenness, debauchery, and general depravity. No child in Tortuga stayed innocent very long, especially if they spent any time down by the bay.

There were only three brothels now, ostensibly operating as 'rooming houses' in a set-aside area behind a butchery, tannery, and stable. The stench there was fairly intense which had likely made the area hard to sell to other more legitimate businesses, though it was something you got used to after a while—especially for those who dealt with fishing or anything that involved ship bilge. Two of the three buildings were quickly thrown together hovels of a couple rickety stories and they all appeared to be occupied if not overly busy.

These brothels seemed to keep strictly evening hours. Some of the upstairs girls had opened their window shutters for some fresh air, for the evening land breeze blowing out toward the bay helped move the stink away.

Jez knocked on the first doorframe and someone came and drew back the canvas curtain still covering it, for this building had opened before it had even been properly finished. "You want to come see what we have inside young Monsieur?" an older creole woman in heavy makeup said as she stuck her head out to look Jez over in the wan light cast from the red-shaded lantern hanging above. She was obviously the Madame in charge, for she was dressed in a tight ruby satin gown with black velvet slippers embroidered in red silk, her graying brunette hair piled in high curls on her head.

Tall and thin, dressed like any successful pirate ashore, Jez probably did look like a young man in the half dark when viewed from within. She got right to the point because she didn't feel like bantering with the woman. "No Madame, I am looking for Capitaine Peter Soloman or a big Negro named Jengo who travels with him. Can you tell me if they are here?"

"*Je suis désolé Mon Cher*, but those men are not here *maintenant*, though we have many lovely young ladies within who would enjoy to sit and talk with you while you wait for you frien's. Maybe you come inside and they will come find you instead—eh? We have beer, ale, and wine and two of my little birds can sing like canaries. You will have such a wonderful time..."

"Not tonight, thank you," Jez said and backed away. She could hear the woman swearing at her in French for being a "*fils de chien bon marché*" as she strode off, and Jez grinned. Her mother had sometimes said that too when someone who looked like he had ample coin to spend had turned up his nose at her establishment and then wandered away without even tipping her.

The next building was far larger and better constructed, so whatever it replaced had likely been well funded and quite popular before the Spanish raid. It was well lighted within and without, but also had a concierge, a burly old sailor in long striped breeches and a sleeveless jerkin showing off his muscular arms covered in gunpowder spot tattoos. He wore a single gold earring, some well earned scars, and had a shaved head. There was a truncheon stuck in his sash. He appeared to be screening who was allowed in. Jez stepped up carefully and eyed him before she spoke.

"Excuse me matey, but I'm looking for some friends of mine. Would you happen to know if Captain Peter Solomon and the big Negro Jengo are within?"

"Who wants te know?" he said with a scowl showing missing teeth, his big arms crossed on his chest. They were both about the same height, but he looked like a mountain and appeared mean enough to use that cudgel on her.

"I'm Captain Johnston of *Revelation*. I heard they might be staying in Tortuga while their ship is in dry dock." Maybe that might jog his memory.

"Mebbe ya heard wrong, Cap'n Johnston," he replied flatly. "If'n ye got no other business inside, then move along." He waved her away.

It was Jez's turn to frown, though she kept the anger out of her voice. "Could I at least come in and look around, maybe talk to some of the ladies?"

He laughed. "Not wit'out paying an entry fee," he said with a superior smirk, though his big right hand was now resting on the end of that club. His left hand went out and she saw he had two missing top finger joints. "That'd be two silver coin or ye go yer way and stop botherin' me."

"That's piracy ashore!" she said with a growl. As he began to pull the club free, Jez backed off with her hand on her hanger. "Nobody in Tortuga charges a fee to simply come inside!"

"Well, we do now, ye mouthy whelp. Pay up fer wastin' me time, 'cause it be better'n me brainin' ye here and leavin' ye for dead. And doncha pull that pig sticker on me lad, ye'll not live long enough te regret it."

Jez had enough of his attempted extortion by then, so she had drawn her hanger and had it firmly in hand. She crossed it before her in a guard position, when another man came to the door.

"What is the all the fuss about Jacob?" he asked. This portly fellow was well-dressed in flashy gold on green brocade suit with an orange lining and frothy lace, so he appeared to be wealthy. *Was he a client or an owner?* Jez wondered.

Sailor Jacob turned to the man and spoke quite respectfully. "We have here some young fella as wants in fer free to jist look 'round for his frien's. When I told him we has an entry fee, he got himself edgy-like and pulled his blade on me."

"Well, we certainly cannot afford that sort of notoriety," the man said as he came closer to gawk at Jez. He was a bit short sighted for he was wearing round spectacles that hung by a silken cord at his neck which he pulled up to his eyes. Then his mouth went wide. "I say, aren't you the lady captain who brought her entire crew ashore and helped us clean up and rebuild?"

"That's me, Captain Jezebel Johnston of the good ship *Revelation*," Jez answered with a smile as she sheathed her sword and gave him a slight bow. "I recognize you now Sir, you're the man who owned the big mercantile up the line—or what was left of it when we got there," she said.

"I am he, yes. Horace Manfred at your service Captain Johnston," he said with a courtly bow that would have dropped his spectacles had they not been on that cord. He turned to a now aghast Jacob the concierge and said, "Oh don't just stand there looking bewildered man, let her inside! We will always wave that entry fee for Captain Johnston, she's a blessing to those of us who lost our buildings in the Spanish bombardment. With her influence and her sterling example, the other captains in port brought their men in as well, and then the Governor and his prosperous cronies up in the hills were rather shamed into sending down some of their plantation workers to pitch in alongside them. So, the cleanup and the reconstruction got done far faster. Plus, we didn't have to pay for every little thing in order to get something rebuilt." He was smiling broadly. "Oh, do please come in Madame Captain, I am sure our ladies would love to meet you."

"Um... all right, though I am actually here searching for some old..." Jez just could not say 'friends' again—not when thinking of Sol anyway, for he had made her early shipboard life difficult. So, she quickly changed that to, "shipmates that I hear are in port. If your ladies would be kind enough to say if they saw these two men, and where they might now be, that would be much appreciated. I have some business with them."

"Oh, most certainly Captain Johnston," Horace Manfred said as he led Jez inside what he called his 'salon'. This was a high-class establishment for a bordello, with well-appointed decor, and the women sitting around were all properly dressed and did not appear as tawdry or sadly hollow-eyed and hopeless as were most port whores. Obviously Master Manfred had found himself a lucrative new business venture and unlike most brothel owners, his women seemed to adore him.

If there were any customers, they were already upstairs.

As it turned out, Sol had been there earlier in the day, but he also was simply looking for someone else, and it was a name that Jez did not recognize. It made sense that Sol wouldn't do any business there, for admittedly *Aphrodite's Pearl* as the place was named, was quite expensive and catered to a higher class of clients. That it had to be located down by the harbor in such a wretched neighborhood bothered old Horace to no end, but rules were rules. It was clean and the women seemed well cared for and as happy as any working whore gets, so Jez did not question his choice in a new business.

Who this mysterious *Monsieur Corbeau* was that Sol had been looking for; a man whose name was spoken of in whispers, she would have to find out. The women did not know if Jengo was involved, for they had not seen anyone fitting his description with Captain Solomon. The story seemed to become even more convoluted when she stopped at the final of the three brothels, whose madam was a slattern with a warty nose who said she thought the nigga had been in but that was a few days ago. Jez got a quick look inside that place, and it turned her stomach, for most of the girls were colored or otherwise of mixed race and all were quite young. A few of them had open sores or bruises, some of which may have been due to the braided leather switch the old hag carried. They were barely dressed, if at all, their hair filthy and stringy, probably crawling with lice. This was a disconsolate and pitiable group, some of them younger than Jez had been when she first went to sea.

This was no life for a female of any age, but especially not for girls too young for woman's blood. Why Jengo would find that sort of slavery appealing enough to visit this pigsty made Jez wonder what kind of man he had turned into since last they had served aboard together.

She would be heading back to her ship a lot later than she had expected to. Since the harbor was quiet at night and there was a rising crescent moon, Jez initially rowed down past the dry dock to have a quick look at the brig that Sol was supposedly having rebuilt. Even in the dark, she could tell that whatever wood that the shipworms hadn't gotten to first was old and dry rotted. Maybe the keel and some of the frame might be salvageable but that was an awful lot of trouble to go through just to make something seaworthy. It would be far more lucrative to either buy a better ship or capture one. Most of what was going on with Sol and Jengo made no sense to Jez at all.

While rowing herself back to *Revelation*, her mind was in a muddle. Where in Tortuga were Sol and Jengo staying, and how were they affording to pay for it as well as fixing up an old tub like that? Was Lévesque paying for all this, or did he have friends on Tortuga who were hosting his followers? These were things Jezebel Johnston felt impelled to find out some way.

After stopping at the harbormaster's shack to give Antonia's message to the drowsy fellow on guard, Jez made it back to *Revelation* just before midnight. Since they were anchored stern toward the harbor, they had left an aft lantern lit for Jez, and she only had to 'ahoy the ship' to bring a man from the watch running as she tied the crew boat off to one line and then walked up the stern with the help of another one he threw down and clambered over the taffrail.

"Leave the crewboat down there for tonight lad, we'll have time enough to move it come morning," she told him as she strode across the quarterdeck and headed down the ladder to her cabin below. "I'm going to get some closed eye time in my bunk, for tomorrow will be a busy day. Let the morning watch know to make ready to weigh anchor and unfurl the turning sails for we'll be moving her up to the docks for unloading."

"Aye aye, Mum," he said solemnly while saluting, and she winced. They trained these English Navy fellows to bow and scrape to everything. Jez was too tired to care at the moment, but she would address the crew at how to act like pirates before they made it to the docks come the morning. It would be best not to put on any shows that would lead to further conjecture as to where they and their ship had originated.

She fell into her narrow bed still half dressed, for the call to the deck would come early on the morrow. Jez was asleep only moments after her head hit the thin pillow.

Her Italian quartermaster certainly loved the ship's bell because Beppe rang it for every watch as well as to call men to their stations. That bell ringing and the dawn light streaming into her open casement window is what awakened Jez. She wanted very much to turn over and go back to sleep, for the few hours she'd been able to snatch after getting back so late were not enough. Yet duty called and so she sat up with a yawn and a stretch, and began lacing on her boots and making herself presentable. Once the ship was snugged up to the dock, she would be up and down all day, first down in the hold making sure that things were properly bundled for removal and placement on the wagon, then out on the dock directing which bits must go first.

She had not forgotten Antonia's low-voiced suggestions not to tie up dock space for too long or they would draw the sort of attention to themselves that would not prove favorable. Jez had scouted the new docks while she had been down there and decided to choose one closest to the far end that would be sufficiently long and large enough for her ship. It was often used by fishermen to tie up at night, but at this time of day it should be gradually opening up as the boats went out. It was a bit cramped in that area and the bay was not as deep there, but *Revelation* was a smaller ship with a somewhat shallow draft that gave it the ability to carefully slip up. Plus, her lads were not a bunch of drunken louts but a hardy lot who knew their business; that she could always trust.

When she was back on deck, the sun was above the horizon and the air already warming. Jez could feel the excitement all around her and she smiled. Men were singing at the capstan while they hauled anchor, and others in the rigging had joined in on the choruses as they began to untie reefing lines so the pertinent sails could be unfurled for turning and tacking. Beppe stood on the quarter deck calling out orders that were shouted from one station to the next, so she headed up to join him.

"*Buongiorno Capitana!* It look like a fine day for unlading, sì?"

"That it does," she admitted, glancing at the harbor around them and checking the angle of the sun on the horizon. It was still early enough in the day that the first string of fishing boats were just heading out past them. There weren't too many larger ships at anchor that they would have to dodge to get to where they would dock and with most of the debris gone from the harbor bombardment, they should have an easy enough time of it.

The less problems they caused the people of Tortuga, the better. Jez now realized she was a stranger here, and as a pirate she would be watched closely. This had to go well.

As if reading her thoughts, Beppe asked, "All is fine ashore then?"

"As fine as it can be," she answered without going into detail. "I want to get this ship unloaded and then we will go back to a harbor anchorage. We'll give the lads aboard a short time in town to enjoy themselves, but they can't get too wild about it. There are new rules here since the bombardment, so that explains why things are so quiet. This used to be primarily a pirate port, but not so much anymore."

"We have been to other places where there was little of what the English called 'liberty time'. Or sometime we were in a foreign land where certain ways of acting ashore were not allowed. I will speak to them, and they will behave well, or next time they stay on board."

"Thanks Beppe, I would appreciate that. I have a lot on my mind right now so it's one less thing I will need to deal with."

"Is nothing," he said, waving a hand. "But Jez, where is de little ship with your friend? Should they not be here by now?"

That was something Jez had not even thought of, and she slapped her forehead, setting braids filled with beads to clacking together. Where the hell *was* Walter and *Sea Witch*?

"I've been so busy I had not given that much thought. They weren't hauling anything too weighty, so once that yard was pared down and fixed in place they should have come in right behind us. I hope he didn't run into some trouble on the way back."

Beppe picked up quickly on the perturbed tone in her voice and he placed a calloused hand on her arm.

"I would not worry too much. I was not thinking dey would be in danger. Such small ships can run fast in shallow water where big ships not go. Most likely, they stop somewhere. You know dey drink very much aboard. Maybe dey run outta rum."

"Aye, maybe," Jez said in a sour tone, thinking of how close Port Royal Jamaica was when they left the area around the Spanish Main. That was the big booming pirate port in the Caribbean these days that Walter had somewhat raved about. From all accounts Jez had heard from other pirates, things were incredibly expensive there. What *Sea Witch* had aboard was supposed to go directly to Antonia Campos for her shop though—that was the agreement they both had made. If Walter had squandered all or even most of their share of the plunder so that he and his much wilder crew could have a fine time ashore, Jez would make her displeasure known and she would see that he personally explained to both Antonia and his mother what he had done. *Sea Witch* had originally belonged to Lucien Lévesque until her former captain Émile Gagnon sailed off with it. Since Émile was now dead, in Jez's mind that made it Antonia's ship and Walter's responsibility to bring in a cargo. He would have to make amends with her if he had squandered his part of the prize.

It could also be that Walter had simply decided to take what he had aboard and move on, now that Jez and her crew were working for Antonia. That possibility she liked least of all.

Jez shook off those unpleasant thoughts, for *Revelation*'s anchors were now both catted aboard and her sails were snapping full and catching the wind as the ship was starting to move into a wide turn. They'd be heading toward the docks shortly, so she had to make sure Beppe and the lads knew where she wanted to tie up.

"Starboard tack once she comes full about Beppe. Make for the end of the pier over on the far eastern side." She pointed to the area and they both squinted into the sun. "We'll take her to halfway up that longest dock. There should be enough water there even at low tide that we won't be in danger of bottoming out."

"Aye Capitana," he said, and almost gave a salute again, though he caught himself in time. Jez had made it plain that the less they looked like a bunch navy deserters, the longer they would all live free.

It took the better part of an hour to maneuver around and between ships and then up to the dock in question. There were plenty of onlookers by then, as some of the locals and other pirates ashore got curious about what this small but sturdy English built ship was going to unload. Jez had been down in the hold with the men bundling cargo to be unloaded onto the dock but she hustled back up to the weather deck as soon as she felt the ship turn in and begin to snug up. She wanted to be the first one off in case someone had to speak to the harbormaster. Beppe and the lads could handle the rest aboard, they'd done their share of dock work before.

Fortunately Antonia had already sent down the cargo wagon and team with Jobah driving and the two men who helped move shipments into her warehouse along for the ride. It was parked above the boardwalk area with the duo who would be loading the wagon sitting in the small patch of shade it threw. They had added high sides and moved the driver's seat and spring assembly up accordingly so Jobah could see all around him, so he had not bothered to clamber down and join them. The elderly Negro still sat well up on his high perch with his usual floppy hat pulled down low over his eyes along with one of Antonia's older faded parasols that she had given to Jobah's wife Hetty shading him from the worst of the beating sun. The two younger men by the wagon got to their feet and rapidly headed Jez's way as they saw her making her way across the dock surface, so she strode over to confer with them while Jobah slowly and carefully brought the wagon around and headed down toward the land end of the dock. Jez spoke in a low tone to these trusted employees, for there were too many others nearby, gawking at her ship.

"Lads, much of what is coming off first is fine furniture and household goods. It's prepacked for shipping so well wrapped and all, but you can't be cramming it in too tightly. We don't want it all scuffed or anything broken because these are things that will sell well to the nobs at a steep price. Plus, it was not an easy cargo to come by if you catch my drift..." She let that sink in and they both grinned and nodded.

"Too bad this dock is so blasted narrow, for this would go faster if we could back the wagon over it and load directly. Looks like a damnable long day ahead to me," the big man with the beard said with a wistful sigh. The tall skinny one just shrugged and snorted.

"Yet one you will both get paid well for, regardless of the effort involved," Jez pointed out. "If that shop doesn't fill up, nobody profits and you'll soon be looking for work elsewhere."

"No worries, Ma'am," the bearded one answered with a quick smile. "Mistress Antonia is a fine lady, and she takes care of her own, so we do all we can for her. It's just that we sorely miss Master Émilien, who had a way with others that would have gained us extra hands to load and unload. We'll get it all done though."

"My crew will help out wherever possible," Jez promised. "I just wish we had a second wagon and team." The one they had was coming in close so the two men hustled off to begin loosening the cargo netting and moving the first bundles. Jez also scurried out of the way as Jobah expertly backed the big horses so that the wagon tail would be right at the shore end of the dock, which was as far as he dared go. The elderly man was past the years where he could do much in the way of heavy lifting, plus repeatedly getting up and down off that high seat would not be easy without taking the chance of a fall. He would stay with the wagon while others loaded the cargo and tied the bundles down securely.

Beppe now had the davit crane—which had been previously used to safely cat the anchors without holing the ship—set in place to lift the heavier items out of the open waist deck hatch. Some of the crew were tying thick and wide planks with transverse cleats to the lower, unrailed starboard waist gunnel while others extended them downward to the dock. Those would be used to walk the smaller items down and for quick access to those who needed back aboard. At least they'd get the hold emptied faster that way and could spare some men to help stack things on the dock and load the wagon.

Jez was itching to help as well, but as captain it would be best if she simply stayed out of the way and ready to intercept any potential inquiries or head off problems. She knew her men would not expect her to be involved anyway, though she always did her share aboard whenever possible. The crewmen were in a merry mood, knowing that if they could successfully get *Revelation*'s hold unloaded early today, anybody who could be spared would get immediate 'shore leave' as they termed it. Once the ship was back at anchor in the bay, the rest would go ashore on a rotating basis with watches left aboard. They were good lads and had been patient and willing to learn the pirating business, so they had certainly earned that much.

After suggesting to Paddy that if any men could be spared they be stationed on the dock to undo the cargo netting from lifting items through the hatch and help carry loads to the wagon, Jez tromped back ashore to speak with the wagon driver.

"Jobah," she called up to the dark skinned elder man on the high wagon seat, "I have a suggestion that might speed things up a bit with this." He put down the parasol and raised his slouch hat up to listen better. "When you take Antonia's men back to the warehouse after this first trip, just have them unload the wagon outside and leave them behind to stow things indoors while you're gone. That way you'll get back here faster. I've got plenty of men down here who can load you up next time."

"Oh, you be so right with that one, Miz Jez," he said politely. "I done tole them fellas that b'fore we left it'd be best they stayed behind and made ready, but they wanted to see yer ship come in. They'd be staying behind this trip, I figure, 'cause it's gonna take some time to move that furniture around."

"That it will, because as I warned them, we don't want it marked up before

"Jobah, I have a suggestion that might speed things up a bit with this."

it's sold. Which reminds me, I know the drive back is fairly long but do try and take it easy as you head uptown." She glanced that way, and something caught her eye. "That road is steep and full of ruts," Jez continued in a half-distracted voice as she squinted at the beach above them.

"Don't my poor back and rump know that too well," Jobah said while rubbing a calloused hand along his spine. "No worries Miz Jez, we'll get everythin' up there in one piece, 'cepting maybe meself."

Jobah laughed at his own joke, and while Jez smiled with him, she was distracted. She had noticed a very familiar person who stood out in the small crowd gathering above them to watch her ship unlade.

"I'm sure you'll do fine as you always do. Right now there's someone else I need to see, so we'll talk again later," she told Jobah and then quickly strode up to where the man she had spotted was standing with others who were discussing the trim little ship being unloaded and joking about women who thought they were qualified to be captains. Yet people actually parted to let Jez through as she stomped up and caught the eye of the big framed, muscular black man in raggedy slops and a tar-stained shirt.

"Well Jengo, it's been a long time since I've seen *you*," she remarked.

He gave her a wary look. "You speaking to me Captain? Maybe you want to sign me on as cabin boy, eh? I can work very hard to make you happy!" It was said in a deprecating tone of amusement and a few men who overheard it snickered, but Jez decided to ignore that.

"Yes, I'm talking to you, and I would have you join my crew in a heartbeat. After all, we need the decks holystoned and swabbed and the bilge pumped," she quipped. When Jengo frowned, she added, "You used to be willing to at least smile at a joke. You don't remember who I am, do you?"

"Should I?" he asked with a belittling laugh that held no mirth. His eyes had narrowed though and his hand was on his belt knife because he was tired of hearing about this colored woman who had her own ship and crew and could work like a man. Jez could see Jengo had a few more scars than she recalled, one of which looked like the glancing tip of a blade had caught the end of his nose, the upper lip, and then the chin below. He wasn't dressed too well ashore either; obviously Sol wasn't doing very good in his own captaincy.

"Who you be wench?" he finally demanded as she stood shaking her head, her arms crossed on her chest. "You look and sound like a woman I might know, but I don' remember one so tall. I mostly like them plumper, so they nice, soft and round when you come down on them." He used his hands to indicate buxom contours. "Don' wanna get jabbed by all them bones stickin' out." Men around him laughed, clapped, and whistled.

"That is enough of that talk Jengo, I'm not one of your port whores," Jez fairly spat the words. She dropped her hands to her hanger at her side and began tapping one foot restlessly. Some of the men made quiet comments but then backed off as the two glared at one another. "You were not this brash when we sailed together aboard *Devil's Handmaid*. At least not when Dandy Dan Abrams was captain. That was my first outing on the account, so I have no idea how you acted before that—or since," she added in a low tone as recognition began dawning in the big man's eyes.

"Wait... You tall enough for sure, but you can't be young Jez, he was a boy! I use to tell Sol that all the time, though he said he knew you was a girl." At her rolling eyes and shaken head he realized that she was. "I guess Sol been right all 'long. How he know that, I never could figure."

Jez laughed and all the tension went out of the chance encounter. "I probably looked like a boy back in those days, but yes, that was me. I signed on as Jez, but my name is Jezebel Johnston, and I've been out asea ever since. I'm now captain of that ship down there," she pointed down at *Revelation*. "That's my crew unloading it. I helped capture it in the East Indies and it was gifted to me by the grateful Maratha Indian warlord I was working for at the time. All those men were former crew, and they signed on with me willingly." It was said in a matter-of-fact tone but with honest pride, and she could see that Jengo was duly impressed. "It's a long story for another time when I've less to do," she added.

"Then you done well." He stepped forward and said in a lower tone, "Look, my apologies Jez, because I din't recognize you right off. You sure did come up in the world girlie," he added in admiration as he looked back and forth between ship, the cargo that was being unloaded, and Jez herself. "Why you come back to Tortuga though? This place be dying for our kind."

"I grew up in Tortuga so it is still my home," Jez said with feeling. "What family I have lives here. Look, I've got to get back down there to watch over the rest of the unloading. Walk with me Jengo and we'll have some time to catch up."

"That be fine by me, I got nothin' better to do right now but jawin' with ye anyway," he said with a deep sigh. Jengo had always been a jolly man aboard for a former slave turned pirate, but now he seemed rather bitter. Jez began to wonder just what was happening with him and Sol as they walked down toward her the dock where her ship was tied off.

The unloading had progressed to the point where the tall wagon was carrying as much as they dared fill it with. Antonia's men climbed up to stand precariously on a small footboard attached on either side of the exterior extensions by cables. They hung onto those cables as Jobah lashed the team of draft horses to get them to pull it up the sandy beach and around the end of the boardwalk to take the main road up to the better part of town.

While the wagon was leaving, men continued to unload *Revelation*'s cargo. Jez spoke first to Beppe about getting the rest of the goods off and piled further down the dock and then asked Jengo if he knew anyone else who had a wagon and team for hire.

"No, we just got in port a few days ago," he said. "We don't come to Tortuga often now; Sol likes Charlie's Town in Bahamas. Lots of small pirates there, and not too expensive to refit and set up."

"Then why is that rotten old tub of his here?" she asked and Jengo laughed.

"You heard 'bout that eh? Sol patched it and had a friend coming this way tow it over here because they got no shipwrights or dry dock in all Bahamas and the entire hull be bad. We had to keep bailing and using the bilge pump, it leaked so much. He wants to make it seaworthy. I tol' him is a waste of time and money, but he's got big dreams. You remember Mouse?"

Jez had to think a moment, and then she nodded. "The rich nob's boy who ran away to sea. Yeah I remember that arrogant little sneak."

"That he be. Mouse got sick of being a pirate and goin' hungry, so he come home to Tortuga. His Dada is back in England for a bit, so grateful Mama take him in and give him much money and nice clothes to stay here with her. Sol and I brought him along and Sol made a deal with Mouse. In exchange for certain items Mouse wants—like rum and tobacco, maybe some cheap trinkets to give a serving girl he wants to bed—Sol is getting some o' the Mama's coin from Mouse to help fix his rotten ship. Sol promise Mouse he will own that ship when is all done. You know and I know is all a lie Jez. Sol never give anybody a fair deal but hisself."

This was interesting! "So why are you still with him Jengo?"

The big man shrugged, his arm muscles bulging. "I ain't anymore, but I gots no other work aboard, 'cept maybe one of Lévesque's ship, and I want nothing to do with *The Butcher*. Still, a man has to eat, and he needs somewhere to call home. Sol was all I had."

She turned and grabbed him by the arms. "Then come work for me!" Jez said eagerly. "There's room for you on my ship. We need a man who knows how to fight and can teach others or lead boarding parties. While my lads are good ones, they were English Navy and this was just a packet ship so they never saw a lot of action. Their captain was an old man, ready to retire. I could really use you and at least you'd get paid and have something worthwhile to do for a change, all on a ship that is in excellent condition."

Jengo began to grin, but Jez needed to know how deep he was in with Sol. "Even if you didn't go out with us on this trip, my friend Antonia and my mother could certainly use the help up the hill at their warehouse shop, which is where this cargo is going, by the way." Jengo's grin became a troubled look as Jez went on and she knew exactly why. "I'll warn you now, they and the shop might need guarding from two men who threatened them a few days ago." She watched him closely for a reaction and got first a guarded look and then a big sigh.

"I am guessing you know it was me and Sol. Was Sol's idea after he come down from bothering Mouse for more money. He went in to talk to them ladies while I keep the men you had down here busy. I din' know the old nigga woman was your mam, don't know if Sol does. He wants to join with Lévesque and become a big hero so he can be captain of his own ship and get a better cut o' the take. Sol make a friend of Lévesque while in town, and he tell Sol to go talk with a Monsieur Corbeau. Corbeau is hard man who is good at killing men slowly to get answers but he tell Sol that he don' kill women unless they cross him. Lévesque had tol' Corbeau that the Spanish gal has some book that he wants, so Corbeau say if Sol gets rough with her to get it, that is fine with him—just don' kill her. So, Sol threaten them, but your Maman, she was ready to fight back—she grab a big knife off the counter and point it at Sol. I see where you get the fire from now."

Jez laughed and so did Jengo, though briefly. Then he said, "Look Jez, I dunno if Sol has the backbone to hurt them, but he is mighty desperate right now because Lévesque has already sailed off to find more men wit' ships. As for me... that was too much, what Sol said to them scared ladies, especially how he threaten the little ones. Sol don' understand what it like to be slave, but I do and I wish that on no one. Since I want no part of any business with Lévesque and his frien's anyway, I left Sol after that."

"So where are you staying now?" she asked him and Jengo laughed.

"I got me a little girl in one of the whorehouses who lets me sleep the night if I can pay for it. She's a young one. The other men beat her 'cause she don' know much how to please them, as does the old witch who runs the place when they complain to her about it." Jez nodded, she already knew which house of ill repute that would be, and she hated that sort of life for any girl. "Me though, I treat her kind and I pay good, so they favor me. But I'm almost outta coin now, I haven't eaten in two days 'cause I give them all what I got. I don't like for her have to suffer so much, she be a quiet little thing and always so sad and scared to see me go..."

His voice dropped off and Jez put a hand on his arm.

"I know the house you speak of; the filthy one run by the woman with the warty nose and the braided switch." Jengo nodded, but his eyebrows went up in surprise. "I get around here too when I need to find someone, and I was looking for you and Sol after what I heard from Antonia and my mother. I can tell you right now that the safest way to get that girl out of there before we leave is to buy her freedom. It's also the most expensive way. If you are sure this is what you want, then give me her name and a description, and I'll find out what it would cost. If I can manage the price I will do it, because I'm pretty sure I can find her someplace safe nearby to stay where she will be treated with more respect and never beaten again. If that all proves possible, whatever I spend will have to come out of your take this time around, but at least you'll know she's safe." The big man's eyes lit up at that.

"You got a deal, Jez." They shook hands over it. "I only know one name for her and that is Carline. She is mix Negro and kinda light, small and skinny, very young and her hair is more brownish, long and curly when clean." He indicated height and hair length with his big hands, so Jengo knew her well.

"Carline. Good, that gives me something to go on. I'll have to go up the hill and see Antonia and my mother when the loading is over, but I'll look into it while I'm ashore tonight. Meanwhile you'll be my guest aboard, so you needn't worry about where you're staying for now. I've got food and rum enough left for all and I'll let the lads who draw the watch know you're a former shipmate who has decided to join us. Most of my men will head into this end of town for the evening, because we only need a skeleton crew to bring her back out and set anchor and sails. You're welcome to sup and sleep out there in whatever comfort we can offer. Be thinking about what you want to do from here on in though, because we'll be going back on the account as soon as Walter and his ship are in port. I hope to have a word with him before we leave, and my crew needs some time to have a little fun."

Jengo did not pick up on the name Walter and Jez didn't elaborate. Maybe he had forgotten most of his former shipmates.

"You always was a good kid Jez," he said with feeling, and they shared a quick friendly embrace. "I can help these men unload today if you tell them is your wish."

"I'd appreciate that very much, they can also use you on the capstan later when the anchor goes down. So yes, I will take you up on that," she said with a smile as they made their way up one of the unoccupied planks to the waist of her vessel. "Come meet my Italian quartermaster and the rest of the lads and then grab something to eat before you get to work. This is a great bunch of jack tars, though they're all former English Navy so only just learning what it is we buccaneer types do out here. You'll like them and I know they'll like you," she added rather hopefully.

It took the rest of the afternoon, but eventually *Revelation*'s cargo was fully unloaded. Jengo was quite a bit of help with that, for after a quick bite of ship biscuit soaked in some bumbo, he worked as hard as he ever had. Jez stayed down on the dock, waiting until Jobah, without Antonia's hired hands, came back each time to watch her men fill the wagon. It took four more loads, the last one precariously packed tight and piled up high to be secured with rope and used netting, but she watched the wagon with its sagging springs go up that hill road one final time with a sigh of relief. Her quartermaster met her down on the dock.

"Your Negro friend, he is good sailor, very strong. He work hard and smile much, no complain at all," he told her. Jez nodded with some relief; she knew that meant Jengo should be readily accepted aboard. They had no colored or black African men at all amongst the original crew. So, while the crew respected her for what they knew she could do from firsthand experience, many still had their own personal prejudices about sharing space with those of darker skin.

"I'm not really surprised to hear that Beppe, because Jengo was always a good man to have around and one we could trust. I'm glad he's signing on willingly. He's been a pirate long enough to know what it's all about as well as how things need to be done aboard. I'll have him working with the lads who haven't done much fighting because he's a beast when he gets a cutlass or a pistol in hand and he's big enough to be intimidating too. Jengo is staying aboard tonight so let him find a berth somewhere everyone is comfortable with. Feed him well and then put him to work as needed. He knows all the ropes, and he always does his share. He's likely signing on with us long-term, so treat him as you would any of our lads and that will give him time to make up his mind. He is a friend, but he will expect no more."

"Good to hear all dat. You be coming back aboard tonight, too?" he asked.

"Likely not," she told him with a shake of her head. "I have to go see my mother and my friend with the shop, and there is some other business I have to attend to. Plus, we'll need to re-supply, so I must arrange for that. I should be back by sometime tomorrow afternoon if all goes well."

"Aye Capitana. You want us to leave the crew boat for you den?"

She thought about it for a minute. "No, I'll probably ride in with one of the bumboats. If all goes smoothly, we're going to leave the next day so we can get back out there soon. Do make sure you get all our lads some time ashore as they wish between tonight and tomorrow."

"What if your udder frien', de one with the little ship, he not come in by den?"

"We leave anyway," Jez said with a brief scowl out at the bay where there was no sign of *Sea Witch* even yet. "We're not waiting around for them beyond the day after tomorrow. We need to fill my friend's shop up to the rafters with things she can sell so that we also get our share of the coin."

Jezebel Johnston strode off unsmiling, heading steadily up that hill well behind the wagon, for she had much to do and not enough time to work it out the way it should be. Signing Jengo aboard would be a boon, for he had plenty of pirate experience and she had always liked him. Still, she had many misgivings about how these next couple of days would go—and then what might happen while she was away again. Plus, she was going to have to spend some if not all of her own share of the take after the resupplying was done on trying to bid for Jengo's young girlfriend's freedom. Which meant she'd have little left to bargain with should she need something while away at sea.

All that made Walter's sudden scarcity increasingly frustrating. She wasn't sure how much *Sea Witch* had aboard, but it became obvious to her as they unloaded today that the little sloop had taken most of the smaller, finer items like jewelry, expensive porcelain, and other baubles that were easy to use as a substitute for coin. Jez was kicking herself for not being able to watch the loading closer, for this had happened while she was busy translating for everyone, making sure the people whose ship they had captured knew what was expected of them. Unfortunately her own lads didn't understand the greed of pirates, who were not always trustworthy where valuables were concerned. Not even with their own brethren, something Jez also had learned the hard way while in the East Indies.

Just where in hell was Walter? Had he already spent the remainder of their prize on himself and his ship of drunken fools? It was beginning to feel like Jezebel Johnston had been betrayed once again.

CHAPTER TWO

W alter Armitage was still in Port Royal, Jamaica, making the rounds with Henry Morgan. The stocky, well-dressed pirate kingpin of the town had sold him Jacques Chagall's ship *Danseuse*, for the price of *Sea Witch* and half of the plunder they had aboard.

"You are actually getting quite a bargain, because I could easily have sold her for twice that much. Yet after all, you were the only man willing to stand up with me against that quarrelsome old buccaneer who used to own it, so it seems fitting," Morgan told Walter when they were signing the document that would make the still sleek but far larger Corvette his own. "I might well owe you my life."

"I think you underestimate yourself Captain Morgan," Walter said with a slight smile.

"We are now business partners," Morgan said as he shook Walter's hand.

He clapped his other hand on the buyer's shoulder. "Call me Henry; it is what my friends call me. I am sure my enemies have far more interesting names for me." They both chuckled at that. "Come, let us go celebrate good fortune and good will." They headed out of Morgan's office and back down to the taverns.

Morgan set quite a jaunty pace, which longer legged Walter had to hustle to keep up with. Men and women along the way called out greetings to the celebrated captain, who smiled and waved in return. He was very well liked here in Jamaica even amongst the planters, merchants, and nobility, so Walter found his new won friendship with the local luminary rather surprising. Suspicious by nature, he wondered why the famed pirate leader, who seemed to covet anything remotely attractive as well as useful, would part with that sleek mid-size vessel he had just sold for what *was* a rather fair price in Port Royal.

He got his answer a bit at a time while they were out drinking a few toasts to his purchase. If there was anything that Henry Morgan loved as much as drinking, wenching, and pirating, it was talking!

"I feel I should confess to you, my newfound friend," Henry said in a low and conspiratorial tone, "about why I traded for that little ship you sailed in here with. You see, I recognized it right off. It was reportedly stolen from Lucien Lévesque, who is one of my chief competitors. We tend to do things far differently, he and I..." He stopped at that point to take a drink and fiddled with one of his rings before continuing.

"Lévesque has been going on about losing that sloop for quite some time now—greedy and temperamental devil-spawn that he is. So, owning it now gives me great pleasure, because I know it will fester like a thorn in his rump. There's no way he'll steal it away from me without calling me out, and that is something he does not want to do. I run this island after all, and most of the men in those ships out in the harbor will readily back me against him.

"Oh, I am not merely boasting about that," he added with a wink when Walter gave him a quizzical sidelong glance. "Those lads all had the chance to go off with Lévesque and his bloody barbarian bunch, had they chosen to," he added. "We all know he stirs up trouble wherever he goes. The man is insane! Those who follow me will have a better life, for while my ideas are equally bold, they are also well planned and executed without unnecessary risks or the bloodshed of non-combatants. Oh, I am a pirate through and through," he struck his chest with a big hand, "so I love me some worthwhile plunder, and I am not afraid to kill whenever I must. Yet I am not a monster like Lévesque, who would kill his own mother for amusement. That vicious streak will be the death of him someday."

Walter had enough of a run-in with Lucien Lévesque in the past that he had to agree Morgan's assessment was basically true. They clinked tankards and drank deeply, and then Morgan went on in a self-satisfied tone.

"I know why he wants it back, because that little Bermuda Rig is also a useful tool for doing some spying on the settlements farther in from the coast. The Spanish are not foolish, for they have moved much of their local wealth well inland. A small ship like that with such a shallow draft can sail up rivers and into shallow areas or through reefs. To me that could prove quite useful indeed for what I have planned."

He did not elaborate on that even when Armitage gave him an interested look but instead took another big quaff of the fine rum they had been drinking and belched before continuing.

"Now a word to the wise my friend..." Morgan went on, changing the subject. He laid a finger alongside his nose and grinned. "That sleek vessel of Chagall's that you just purchased from me has some reputation around here from his own double-dealings. You know the French, you can never trust anything that comes out of their mouths." He threw his hands in the air and laughed. "Old Jacques kept only a few favorites aboard that he trusted and for the rest he signed aboard new men every season—always those who had never served with him or others desperate for a berth. He has been known to cheat the majority of his crew out of some of their rightful take before he dismisses them. Consequently, most of his men were soon broke once in port so they signed on with Lévesque and left Chagall high and dry. While he has been a successful captain, Jacques' policies at times have made that ship you now own a target for his peers. If I were you, I would seriously consider changing the name, maybe getting it repainted, perhaps rearranging the sail pattern a bit. Oh... and I'd lose that figurehead for certain."

"But isn't Chagall dead now?" Walter asked after a big glug of rum, and Morgan shook his head, sending his thick dark curls bouncing.

"Not quite, I am afraid. Like a cat, he's hard to kill. My sources tell me that old buccaneer nearly did die, but somehow he's hanging onto his wretched existence, though they are keeping him asleep most of the time with laudanum. He may eventually pull through this, and I am not the sort of man who has people murdered in their sickbeds. Plus, there are others still out there who won't have heard of our little disagreement, and you might encounter them at some point." He swept a hand dramatically overhead, meaning once at sea. "We would not want your maiden voyage in it to be your last. So do refit it because you have the time, plus you will need to sign on additional crew to operate successfully anyway. Not that I need to tell you your business, of course..."

"Well Henry, I'd listen if you did," a half-soused Walter said, leaning in over the table they were sharing. That got him a broad smile.

"I see you are a savvy fellow as well as loyal. Then allow me to enlighten you..."

He leaned in close. "Walter my lad, you should know by now that I am a wise businessman, because I didn't come to the Caribbean colonies as a wealthy noble. I had to make my own way here. Yet I have done pretty damn well anyway, mainly because I tend to see things as they exist and then plan ahead to how best that can be exploited."

"You've done wonders here in Port Royal Henry," Walter admitted. Morgan was basically running the town if not the entire island.

"Exactly. Now while we both apparently agree that Lévesque is a brutal son of a poxy whore, I can tell you that he does have the right idea. We would all fare better if we come at the Spanish in greater numbers right where they congregate, for even in their settlements they will have gold and silver in abundance. Yet any raid on their colonies or other holdings have to be planned well in advance and carried out properly. Now working alone as you have been doing, you'll simply live from one paltry prize to the next and starve in between. You won't get far that way."

"I can't argue with that," Walter said in a thick voice and Morgan nodded.

"That's why you came looking for me. You were smart to do so," he added with a sly smile while he twirled one end of his mustache. It was midday by then and Morgan was also slurring his words, but his mind still seemed clear. He had stopped talking while a serving wench walked up to set down two more drinks for them, though he absent-mindedly fondled her ample buttocks through her skirt. She quickly moved out of reach before sashaying off and Henry watched her go with a dramatic sigh. "I do so love me a woman with a big round behind, they're so much easier to hang onto when the seas get rough," he said and they both chuckled. Morgan took a big sip of the foaming ale he had chosen for this next round of drinks and wiped his curling mustache before he continued speaking.

"You see Walter, me mate," he was now drunk enough to use pirate vernacular and to wax affectionate, "right here in Port Royal, Jamaica is all the good life that you've been missing out on. You seem like a fine fellow in your prime, so you should experience more of that."

Walter snorted but continued in a low voice. "I would love to settle in here, but Jamaica is an English colony, and I am a wanted man back there." At Morgan's shrug he continued, "They would be happy to hang me, and since there is a hefty price on my head, I dare not settle too long in any one place."

"So, what terrible thing did you do besides pirating to earn that dubious distinction?" Morgan asked him in a low voice.

"You really want to know?" Morgan nodded eagerly so Walter shrugged. "I suppose I have little left to lose as it stands. You see, it all happened before I came out here," Walter began, and then with enough alcohol in his system, he launched into his story. Morgan listened with rapt attention.

"Some years past, when I was younger, more ambitious, and easily influenced, I took myself off to war and became a soldier, thinking I might gain some rank and enough coin to live as I pleased. I was a good shot and lucky, was only wounded twice and neither time seriously. I had left a girl behind that my ambitious parents did not approve of because she was lower class—a nursemaid in the house of a minor noble family. She was plain, but sweet natured. They would not consent to me marrying her, and so we had been seeing each other whenever we could. She had some education before her family fell on hard times, which was why she was hired to care for the children and teach them a little. She wrote to me all the time I was away. Her letters did not reach me very often in the field, so by the time I saw them, sometimes months had passed. I was angry when she told me that the younger brother of the man she worked for had taken advantage of her on several occasions. She could not avoid him, and he threatened that if she didn't allow him such privileges, he would have her fired with no references, which would put her family in the poor house. Eventually she found herself with child, and then she was dismissed anyway."

He shook his head which made it spin, and he rested it in his hands. This was not something Walter Armitage spoke much about.

"Do go on my friend, if you will," Morgan said in an understanding tone.

"It was hard to get letters out from where I was, and I was a proud man so no deserter. So, I wrote back and asked her to hold on, that I would take her in whatever condition I found her and my own family be damned if they thought otherwise. Yet my letter came too late. When my tour was over and I got home, I could not locate her. I found out over time that she had felt so disgraced by both that pregnancy and losing her position—plus not being able to help support her family—that she had taken her own life six months previous. So, she and the child died together and were buried as one in an unmarked pauper's grave before I even saw her letters." He hung his head. It was the first time in many a year Walter had told that story to anyone and he got a sympathetic look for that.

"Ah love... it is always so messy," Morgan said with a nod. "What did you do then?"

Walter's face went hard. He took a big drink and then turned to face Morgan. "I had just come home from war, and had watched too many die needlessly as it was, only to find I had lost everything I had lived for. So, I was out of my mind for a while. I stalked the bastard who had ruined her life for weeks on end until one day I found I had a clear shot, and I killed him like a rabid dog right in the midst of his own family's estate, while they were hosting a garden party. Several of them saw me run off. I stole a horse and headed for the harbor, stowing away at night on a trader coming to the New World colonies. The crew found me and the captain put me to work. Once they unloaded in Barbados I was sold as an indentured servant, but I managed to get away with a few others. I turned pirate after that and never looked back. What else was there for me?"

"A very sad and solemn tale," Morgan said over the rim of his tankard, "but quite similar to others I have heard before. Many of us are out here because we were running from something and looking for a better life elsewhere. That better life is what I've managed to build for myself and for those who take my advice." Henry let that sink in before he went on. Intoxicated or not, he was a master negotiator.

"Now as far as the English here, they know full well with this island being too near the Spanish Main to be defensible for them, 'tis only the pirates of Port Royal that keep it in their hands. They will not look too closely at those who help defend their turf—especially now with Charles the Younger back from exile and sitting on the throne. I hear he spends more profligately than our pirates, mostly on himself and his various mistresses. I would not worry overmuch of the crown's reach here, for while they have installed a governor and his advisors, we freebooters are the real power in Jamaica."

"I'd like to believe that," Walter said with a bleary-eyed nod. "I just don't want to do a hempen jig for lingering ashore too long."

Morgan caught his eye and held it. "I can assure you that you shall not have that final dance with the hangman Walter; not if you listen to and accept my counsel. Now other than what your small crew has spent here, you take whatever you have left in storage from your last trip out and use it to fix up that fast ship you just purchased from me. I'll see that you get enough done at a reasonable price to disguise her. I can even provide you with some additional crew. We have men here littering the landscape who haven't been able to sign on with anyone. Yet all that is contingent on you agreeing to accompany me on a raiding trip I've been signing captains and their crews up for daily, now that Lévesque and his Flotilla of Fools have gone their own way."

"Where would we be heading?" Walter wanted to know, but Morgan shook his head.

"I have to keep that secret for now, but it is a place that is filled with treasure just waiting for the taking." He clenched a big fist as if he could simply grab it. "Only those who sign with me will know what and where once we set sail. I want no tongues wagging about this."

That was easy to understand. Yet Walter had a moment of conscience.

"We freebooters are the real power here in Jamaica."

"I was supposed to bring my ship's part of the take back to Tortuga and turn it over to... the... uh..." he wasn't sure what to call Antonia, "the beloved mistress of its former captain, who was running a suttler shop when the Spanish bombarded the harbor and he was killed. She is desperate to make ends meet now and hold onto what little she has."

"Another very sad tale with a distressed woman at its heart," Morgan said with a shake of his head as he signaled the serving wench to bring them yet another round. "You are quite the romantic, aren't you? Well, unfortunately she is on a French island with a dying port and the economy there is being taken over by wealthy planters with lofty expectations of a grand society. Tortuga as a buccaneer island was winding down and the French were pushing the English aside by the time I got there, which is why I sailed off with so many other hardy men and eventually landed here. Grabbing Jamaica from the Spanish was one of the few worthwhile things Cromwell's Commonwealth accomplished, though they would not have done it without us. I would suggest you start thinking of yourself for a change matey, and let these lovelorn young women find their own way in this world. There are certainly enough of them around to become besotted by—take your pick!"

When Walter frowned, Morgan nodded. "I can tell you are an honorable man who likes to keep his promises. Yet I am sure this woman who managed to enthrall one of Lévesque's former captains will find some other way to make do. Go back later when you are incredibly rich if you still feel that way and you can bring her some of that largess—or bring her back here. But work with me now and I promise you won't regret it."

Henry leaned in again, this time he got as close as he could and whispered something to Walter. "I hear you are pretty skilled with a musket, as any soldier would be. I could really use a man like that for what I have in mind, so do think about it."

They drank the last round in silence and then Morgan left him, but Walter did think about it as he staggered out. He continued to think about it after having a long piss in a gutter, and as he walked around the town to clear his reeling head.

Antonia had Jez after all, who owned her own ship with a crew large enough to adequately supply the shop. Walter had been wanting a change of pace, something much more lucrative and exciting that didn't involve chasing down smaller local ships just to see what little they held. He realized that he and his crew were often drunk more than sober these days, and that would eventually cost them their lives. You could not argue with Morgan's obvious success here in Port Royal—hell, the entire island for that matter. What did he really have to lose by taking on some raid the wily Welshman had in mind?

By sundown, he was aboard *Danseuse* and looking around at what had to be done to refit her. Yes, he should do this while he could afford to, even if he started out with nothing again. That had certainly happened before. At least the basic necessities for sailing had been left behind. Someone had moved his own belongings from *Sea Witch* to the captain's cabin aboard *Danseuse*. The majority of Chagall's things seemed to be gone too—including any personal weapons, maps or charts he might have had aboard. Well, that was to be expected, the latter two were incredibly valuable.

Walter would sleep aboard that night and see Henry in the morning to give him his answer. Jean-Claude and the others, well, they could leave if they felt they had better options, because this ship was his own, he had a paper that said so from Henry Morgan. Walter thought of Antonia and Jez with some regret, and yet also some relief. He'd rather go back and explain when he had some coin in hand and more to brag about than to come sailing into Tortuga's harbor with nothing to show for it but a new ship. Antonia might take that well enough, but Jez would be all over him about it, and he was tired of her arch looks and stern lectures.

Jezebel Johnston was someone he had trained to be a pirate, and she had taken to it well. Yet without his help, that young woman would have either been discovered and put off at nearest port, or she would have died aboard. He lay there in the captain's bunk thinking of the stolen moments he and Jez had once shared with great fondness, though little else. She was just the colored bastard daughter of an English Privateer and a freed slave, not someone you settled down to and made a life with.

At least that's what Walter Armitage told himself as he drifted off into sleep with some hard snoring, though his troubled dreams said otherwise.

Looking at the low position of the sun in the sky, Jez decided to make her stop at the brothel area first, before it got too busy. She assumed that Antonia and her mother would be working at the warehouse anyway with all the new merchandise coming in. Once she reached the rough and rutted road that had the stable at the far end with the butcher's shop and tannery side by side, she set off along that and then passed behind the first two businesses to where the three bawdy houses stood segregated from the more welcomed employers in the lower town.

They were fairly subdued at that time of day, for the more acceptable establishments in front were still bustling with town folk or servants from the well-to-do homes up the hill coming down to make or check on orders. Jez slipped quietly along the back lane. She had dressed casually in breeches, knee boots, and a blousy linen shirt with a lace collar with her leather sleeveless jerkin over it. A maroon brocade scarf held her hair in place and another one acted as jaunty sash where her hanger was sheathed. She still kept a knife handy, hidden within one boot. She looked like any captain or quartermaster ashore on ship business. Still tall and thin with that stubbornly jutting chin inherited from her father and her mother's low voice and dark-eyed glare, Jez could easily pass for a young man even in broad daylight, though she often bound her small breasts to enhance the image. That had often worked to her advantage in various situations. She hoped it did now.

Jez had some coin on her, carefully tucked into her loose shirtfront and padded not to rattle, and hoped that would be enough to buy this young girl's freedom. She knew that such a transaction would be strictly 'cash on the barrelhead', as they often warned her in the smaller taverns where they used old barrels for tables and smaller or halved ones for seating. Brothel owners would also expect to be paid in full before the girl could leave. If what she had on her was not considered enough, it would have to be a down payment until she got an invoice written from Antonia for her share of the cargo's value, which she could take to one of the moneylenders for either a small advance on future sales at the warehouse shop or a promissory note. She was not putting up her ship as collateral against anything though, so if that was all they would consider, Jengo was simply out of luck.

She stopped in the lane outside the third of the brothels she had been to the night before while searching for Sol and Jengo, and sighed. Jez knew just from the attitude she had gotten from the nasty baggage that ran the place that this was not going to be an easy negotiation. Hopefully the woman wouldn't recognize her today. Well, there was no time for second guessing! She strode forward and rapped on the door with her knuckles, using the daytime knock her mother had taught her that most brothels recognized as a signal from those who understood what went on inside. It took two tries but a plump girl with stringy blonde hair and wearing a dingy shift with long stockings cracked open the door a bit and peeped at her.

"Most be sleepin right now. Whatcha wantin' here sailor?" she said with a slight Dutch accent and a lisp, her smile showing missing upper front teeth. She had struck a saucy pose, obviously hoping to pick a little coin on the side without giving the house their due.

"I need to talk some business with your Madam. Could you let me inside to wait?"

"She be knowin' ya then?" The smile was gone with that question and she had turned suspicious.

"She will know me soon enough. I am Captain Johnston of *Revelation*, and I have something important to discuss with her alone. Go wake her please wench, I have much to do this eve, and this is only my first stop."

"I guess ya can come in then," she said and opened the door just enough for Jez to slip though. "Set yaself down and I'll go waken Mam, though she gonna be powerful mad wit' me if'n this be jist a courtesy call to book wit' one of us fer the night. 'Tis first come, first serve in this house. But I'll go get her, though it mought take some time fer her ta get up, she sleeps sound like," the buxom blonde said over her shoulder as she waggled off toward the back rooms.

The place smelled, mostly of sweaty, unwashed bodies, cheap alcohol, and spicy bean soup. Anything inexpensive that would fill a big pot and give everyone a bowl of something once a day was good enough for common whores. Most of the working women were still upstairs asleep, the only other one on the ground floor bedsides the girl who answered the door was a skinny negro of middle age with a club foot, who was snoring on a worn settee in nothing more than a ratty linen smock that you could plainly see through, the kirtle that had covered it bunched up beneath her head. She never even woke up when the newcomer walked into the room.

Jez didn't bother to sit down, the furniture did not appear very clean, and cushions were likely filled with lice and fleas. There were big roaches scuttling across the worn carpeting, looking for stray bits of dropped food. She managed to stomp out a few with her boots while restlessly pacing back and forth, waiting with growing impatience for the madam to pull herself together. Jez had to admit, as much as she hated the business, her mother's brothel had been run far better that this pigsty of depravity.

When the woman she had spoken to the night before finally showed up, she was a bit bleary-eyed but dressed well enough to be passably tidy. Her skirt was worn and faded ruby red satin but filled out her scrawny body due to a bumroll along with a puffy sleeved chemise and a couple of stiff petticoats. The heavily boned and tightly laced bodice shoved her meager bosom up high into the off-the-shoulder neckline. Her dull red hair had been hastily piled up in greasy coils and she wore inexpensive, though flashy, jewelry. A bit of face powder and a splash of lavender water did little to disguise her age or fetid body odor. Jez was used to sweating men aboard ship, but this woman smelled like she hadn't bathed in many years!

She also had the shakes of the habitual tippler, and her dull blue eyes showed the pinpoint pupils notable amongst opium smokers or laudanum abusers. Jez suspected the latter, for laudanum as a medication was basically a tincture of opium infused in alcohol, at least the way Dottie of Libertalia fixed it. It would be cheaper to get and easier than smoking.

"I am Madam Lenore, and this is my house. What can we do for you today, Captain Johnston?" she said in a far softer tone than she had used the night before. Jez doubted the bleary-eyed woman even recognized her. She sounded like English was her usual language.

"I have something important that I wish to discuss, if you have some place where we can speak in privacy," Jez answered, keeping her voice down and low.

The woman sighed. "Of course, come back to my office," she said before turning an eye to the chubby blonde. "Mia, go awaken the others for the evening company hours," she commanded, and the eavesdropping girl clomped upstairs after shaking the clubfooted one on the couch to some semblance of wakefulness.

The office was a small table and a couple of straight-backed chairs in an alcove. It was far from private, for the kitchen area was nearby, but nobody seemed to be stirring in there at the moment.

"Now what exactly did you want to talk with me about, my tall young gallant of the seas?" the warty-nosed woman said with an ingratiating smile as she plumped down in one chair. Jez took the other one across from her after running a hand across the seat to knock some debris off. So far she seemed to be pulling off her disguise as a man. She removed her purse from the shirt front and set it on the table next to her.

"I am here to buy one of your women," Jez told her, crossing a booted ankle over her knee and leaning back a bit as she had seen men do. The woman across from her gave her a strange look and then a smirk. Fanning herself with a hand, she pursed her rouged lips.

"Why I had no idea that I have anyone up for sale. This isn't an auction house after all." Her tone was now far less polite and far more informal.

"Isn't it?" Jez said with a raised eyebrow. "Don't those girls go to whoever bids highest on them each night?" At the woman's frown she unfolded her leg and with both boots flat on the floor, leaned forward and laid crossed arms on the table. "You're not at all curious about which one?"

The woman gave her a sneer of contempt, all pretense at polite speech now gone. "Naw, just wonderin' why you pretend to have a care for a common whore. These girls aren't your sort of choice, a dashing young captain like yourself will want what's next door at Horace's more genteel salon. My doxies are for the common sailors with more busting out of their slops than they have in their purses or heads." At Jez's frown, she continued, "Look, I know what I have to offer here. They're all I can afford. Find yourself a favorite elsewhere that isn't going to give you the clap or crabs. These girls are the worst on the island for that."

"The one I am looking for is a young girl, named Carline," Jez continued, ignoring the house madam's frank speech. "One of my crew fancies her and I'm buying her so he can keep her as he pleases and not have to come back to find her all battered and bruised."

That's when things got heated. She gave Jez an arch look. "You tell that big nigga that Carline ain't for sale at no price," she said getting to her feet. "She already got her a regular man sponsor anyway, and I'm not disappointing a paying customer by selling his favorite out from under him. This meeting is over, sir—goodbye!"

Jez had been afraid this was the way things would go. She got to her feet too but leaned forward again with her hands on the table. "How much does Carline's sponsor pay for her each visit?" she demanded, looking down at her full purse.

"That is none o' yer goddamn business!" she retorted, pushing past Jez. "Now leave b'fore I have you removed."

"Oh, and who would do that? There's no guards down here and they wouldn't come to your whore house anyway, unless a man more flush with coin than most of your customers complained or someone got killed," Jez replied coldly as she picked up her purse and tucked it back into her shirt.

"The latter circumstance could be arranged easily enough," said a familiar snide and ill-tempered voice from behind Jez that made her whirl with her hand on her hanger's hilt. It was Sol. He was skinnier than she remembered with a drooping eyelid that plainly showed it had been restitched into place—likely from a close call with a blade or something else sharp. He also had some missing teeth and dark gums due to scurvy. His clothing was cheaply made and tar stained as well. So, he hadn't done well enough on his own to even own one proper outfit for being ashore.

He noticed her taking stock of him and grinned, scratching his stubbly chin with ragged, tar-stained fingernails.

"Well, well, well... if it isn't the famous Captain Johnston. Welcome back to where you started Jez, it's all downhill from here," he said with a sarcastic snarl as he whipped out a rusty saber he'd picked up somewhere cheap to use as a city hanger and pointed that at her. "Saw you down by the small docks earlier talking to that turncoat Jengo and I wondered where I'd find you next. I have to admit, it wasn't in here that I figured you'd be." He stepped forward a pace but stopped because she had whipped her own blade out and held it in a guard defensive position.

"I thought something smelled like a well-known traitor when I stepped inside, but I figured it was just an overused slops bucket," she said with an even tone and a scowl. He laughed.

"Always playing pirate, ain't you girl? By the way, in case you're wondering," he continued, ignoring the brothel madam's squawk of terror as she struggled to push her way past him before they came to blows, "I'm the one that owns little Carline's skinny ass now." He thumped his chest with his off hand's thumb. "And I intend to break her in properly. So, if Jengo wants her, he can come deal with me. Tell him I said he needs to find his balls instead of sending some girl pretending to be a captain to do his fighting for him. You I can take out easily enough; with him it'd be a far fairer match."

"Maybe you want to test that theory?" Jez said evenly with a practiced flourish of her own sword, a much finer and better-kept weapon than he owned. "I've fought men far more skilled than you'll ever be, Sol. And I daresay far more of them too." It wasn't idle bragging on her part, but Sol laughed anyway.

"What did you do—stab them while you were flat on your back in bed and they too busy grinding away at you? Because that always seemed to be your best chance of securing a berth aboard or any other favors you wanted."

What Jez wanted very badly at that point was to wipe the nasty smirk off his face, but she knew Sol was baiting her. He was hoping she'd come at him in anger so he could just gut stab her and be done with it. He'd seen her fight before and he knew in a more protracted battle; she was faster and more surefooted than he would ever be. Jez would love to run him through as well, but she'd rather take it outdoors where there was more room to move. She was about to suggest that when the madam came back with a couple of big sailors who were getting a free hour with the girl of their choice that night in exchange for tossing these two out the door.

"Sheath them blades ya biscuit eaters and leave now. There be no fighting in the bawdy house or ye'll bring the watchman and any other bystander he can drag along down on us all," one of them said as they both endeavored to separate the two grimacing pirate captains. These men were both armed with carved whalebone marlin spikes, and like any sailor, they knew how to use them as weapons. This could quickly become a free-for-all.

Sol was grinning as he gradually lowered his weapon. Jez sheathed her sword and yanked herself free of the man who had laid hands on her, pushing past them all before stalking away toward the entrance. She didn't want any trouble in Tortuga—not if she was going to help Antonia and her mother. Yet ever cocky Sol stood his ground, and he turned to stare the two men down.

"You lads don't want a visit from Corbeau do ya? He owns this wretched place now and Corbeau don't take kindly to fellas as interferes with his business partners. Down this end, he be the true law and he'll soon own most of this dirty little corner. He put me in charge here, so what I say goes."

That was interesting to hear, and it stopped her in her tracks. Unfortunately the madam was giving her the fisheye that said she'd better leave, and now. As she hustled out the door, Jez noticed that Sol remained behind. She waited a bit to see if he would follow her, and when he didn't, she surmised he was staying behind to let everyone know he was in charge from here on in.

What had Sol done for this Corbeau person that gained him that privilege?

She wandered over to *Aphrodite's Pearl* next. Since it was early, there was no doorman. She knocked, and Horace Manfred answered the door himself.

"Just the man I wished to speak with," she said with a smile.

"I say lad, we're not open until sunset when the lanterns can go on. New town rules and all that..." At her chuckle he placed his spectacles up on his nose and then exclaimed, "Oh, forgive me. Captain Johnston, I did not realize it was you! Do come in, I'm sure the girls would be more than happy to see you again."

"Thank you, I'd appreciate that, because I ran into some trouble next door that I thought I should warn you about." She pointed toward the brothel she had just come from.

"Oh my! Well then, please come and sit with me instead, for I would very much like to hear all about it," he said and then beckoned her to follow him. He escorted her to a smaller private salon in the back where he indicated any piece of furniture in the room. "Do make yourself comfortable." She took a seat at one end of a divan. A well dressed and coiffed young woman came swishing up and Horace said," Miriam, bring us some wine. Perhaps the port, it's a fairly new shipment. And see that things go well out front, we should not be disturbed here other than for perhaps some nibbles." The woman smiled and nodded before she headed off. Horace turned back to Jez and sat down opposite her.

"Miriam is a fine hostess, she worked in a manor as a governess for a few years before moving to the colonies as an indentured servant. There's a long story there, but in the end, I paid dearly to liberate her for I could see she had manners and good breeding and only needed a second chance. She has learned well from me. Now what can I help *you* with Captain Johnston?"

"Well first of all you can call me Jez like everyone else does," she said as another girl who was obviously kitchen help, came in with a tray of small cakes along with other tiny savory pastries and sugared confections. She set them down nearby and began to arrange them until Horace clicked his tongue and motioned her off. Jez had waited as patiently as possible until the girl left, for she wasn't sharing her business with the drudges, who loved to gossip about the 'grand folks'.

"All right then, Jez, then you may call me Horace, since we are now good friends. First though, let us have a sip and enjoy a treat or three and then you can tell me what troubles you today."

What he really meant was let's not talk further until my people have left the area. Miriam came back next with the wine and two lead crystal goblets while they were munching on things. He nodded and she set them down within reach on the small table nearby and then left. Horace heaved himself back up to shut the door and then saw to the rest.

"I think you'll enjoy this wine, for it is strong and sweet—that is providing I can get this damnable cork out, if you'll pardon my vulgar tongue," he added while struggling with trying to pop it. "It's a new way of keeping wine fresher on long voyages, they pour wax over the cork which you must peel off first and then pull the cork itself. Yet that wax sinks into the cork and makes it so... so... slippery..." He had covered it with his handkerchief but was turning rather red from exertion of trying to alternately twist and pry it loose.

"May I try Horace?" Jez said, and he handed it over. The cork had a top knob, which she gripped in her hand tightly and gave it a wicked twist. There was a pop, and it pulled free.

"You embarrass me with your strength I fear," he said with a self-deprecating laugh as he took the bottle from her, but then Jez showed him her hand.

"It's the calluses," she told him with a wink. "I will never be a drawing-room-proper lady, but then, I run a ship and there's so much rough work aboard that this is the result. We all have our strengths and our weaknesses I suppose."

"Indeed we do," he agreed as he poured for them both, once the wine had settled. He handed her a glass and then sat back down with his own drink, ran it under his nose and sniffed it, then took a sip and sighed happily. "Finally, a refined libation! I do so tire of ale and rum." He turned to Jez and saw her sipping hers with pleasure and that made him smile. "Now tell me, Captain—er, ah—Jez, what exactly troubles you this eve?"

Jez really liked Horace Manfred, who treated her like an equal, something she had not experienced very often in her life. She opened up, quickly apprising him of her day, the chance meeting with her former shipmate, Jengo's concern for the young prostitute next door, and then her own attempt to buy the girl's freedom from her madam. Having Sol appear saying he owned the girl now and that Corbeau had bought out the disgusting brothel and partnered with Sol made Horace frown. Yet he let her finish her tale before he commented, pouring them both a second glass.

"I must say Jez, you do have your adventures—even ashore. I am vaguely familiar with this Corbeau character, though strictly by reputation alone. He seems to be some friend of that dastard Lucien Lévesque, for Corbeau sailed in with Lévesque and then set himself up as a businessman, though why in this area and what business he pretends to have, I've no idea. He seems to be independently wealthy, so in my estimation he would be better served moving into the uptown area, as would my establishment, though perhaps the elite do not wish either of us to be part of their section of town. He does have a rather nasty reputation as an assassin."

"So I have heard," Jez said in a sour tone, though she was grateful for all that Horace knew about the mystery man. "Well at least my friend and former shipmate will now sail with me rather than take up with someone like Lévesque. Yet he worries about this little one that he has some affection for. She is very young, of mixed blood, so likely has nowhere else to go. That place is filthy, and all the girls look sick or ill-used. He says she has been often beaten because she is not very skilled at... what they want her to do. Jengo said she is barely out of childhood, so no wonder there. If I can get her removed from that hellhole, he agreed to sail with me and is willing to take less of his share of the profits when we get back into port. She means that much to him. He's an excellent fighting man; I could sorely use him."

"I see," Horace said with a distant look. "Perhaps I can help here, for we could use some simple assistance in the way of maid service, if she would be up to that. Nothing too heavy... just aiding the girls with getting dressed, changing linens as they become soiled, maybe at times serving drinks or comestibles whenever our main salon is open. I have my ladies rotating at those duties now, as you saw today. In exchange she will be well fed and dressed appropriately and she'll have her own little cot up in the attic with the other servants. The men who come here have manners and most of them are from good families, so even well into their cups they are not the sort who grab at our staff. We do not offer children for their pleasure, and they know this, and we will deny anyone entrance who is not on our guest list. So, she would be far safer with us, I daresay."

This was more than Jez had hoped for, and with the fortified wine hitting her on an empty stomach, she turned a grateful look on Horace Manfred.

"That would be a great load off my mind, providing you don't mind my shipmate asking after her. He is a full Negro, a former slave and has been a freebooter ever since he gained his freedom."

Horace thought about that a moment, his double chin propped on one hand with his head tipped to one side, the elbow propped on the divan's arm. He took another sip of wine from the goblet in the other hand, and then his face brightened.

"Well, seeing as she will be a servant here and not one of my ladies of pleasure, I am sure we could arrange something for them, though *how* to do that is a question I must ponder further. Yet if you have no problem with me owning her and perhaps seeing that as she matures, she gets some education as well as training in the classic art of a courtesan, I will make inquiries of both that disagreeable harpy next door and then if necessary, the infamous Monsieur Corbeau. He knows who my clientele are or he would have paid me a visit by now. I rather expect we could work something out to purchase her freedom from that despicable establishment. By the way, do you know what the girl's name is?"

"Carline," Jez said, getting back on her feet. "A small girl who is barely in womanhood. I'm told she is thin, shy, and full of bruises."

"Ah Carline, *that* is a lovely name! Oh yes, this could work out well for all of us. And her protective lover?"

"Jengo, a big and burly man, black as the night. But a good soul or I'd not take him aboard."

"Oh yes, he was one of the two you came here looking for."

That reminded Jez of Sol's claim. "I should warn you, I had a run in with the man who Jengo was previously working for. We know him as Sol, but he now calls himself Captain Peter Solomon, I guess because he owns that old wreck of ship in the dry dock down at the harbor. They both sailed in on that with someone towing it. Sol now claims to own the girl, he said Corbeau gave her to him when he made him a partner in the brothel. Sol wanted her specifically because Jengo cut ties with him and took up with me instead."

Horace frowned a bit at that. "Well that might make her price somewhat steeper than I had hoped for." When Jez took out her purse, he shook his head and bade her put it away again. "No, that is not necessary Jez. We are doing quite well here, and I am the one who is buying the girl, which I assure you that I can well afford. I am just worried more about how to allow them time together, because..." He hesitated and then went on.

"You see Jez, my establishment caters to those of fair skin only, though the men who come here have no qualms about spending time and coin on well-groomed and properly behaved women of color. To pull this off we would have to smuggle your associate in the back way, and then I will have to see if we can arrange for them to have some privacy. I'll work on that while you are out at sea. For now, you tell this man Jengo that if he can be patient and abide by my rules, his little love will be very well-cared for. Should she decide to join my other charming Pearls once she is of age, he will need to share her company only when she has a day off. I assure you that none of them are prisoners here, they come and go as they please outside of business hours. In the meantime, your associate must work hard and save some coin to buy her freedom back if he wishes to have her all to himself—I will only charge him what I paid, no interest. That is the best deal I can offer, but I am a fair man; one who protects his employees and will work with those who have treated us with equal respect.

So, I will consider any other reasonable counter offer." He stuck out his right hand.

It was better than Jez could have done on her own, so she shook hands with him. "You know Horace, it is a pleasure doing business with you," she said with feeling. "You would have made an excellent trader, better than many I heard of in the East Indies."

"Oh, you so flatter me Captain Johnston," he said with a chuckle and his soft brown eyes sparkled. "Frankly, I consider myself more of the pirate type, though I would never survive on the open ocean. I get dreadfully seasick, and I tend to avoid physical labor as well as dangerous confrontations. I do so admire you for your bravado and fortitude though—especially as a woman! I suppose you could call me a land pirate." Then he leaned in close and raised a cautionary finger.

"Because I trust and respect you, I will take you into my confidence. You see Jez, while this is a French island with some rather hostile Spanish neighbors, this Englishman is an ambitious fellow," he jabbed a big thumb into his chest, "who intends to own a good portion of the town before I have 'shuffled off this mortal coil' as the Great Bard William Shakespeare phrased it. I did not just randomly decide to open a high-class den of vice you know. I saw no better way for an industrious entrepreneur like myself to get to know the male gentry well. These men are wealthy and well-connected; they have most of the power here, and all have knowledge I can plumb as well as weaknesses that can be carefully exploited. Do you think me ruthless for saying so?"

"No more than I am, Horace," she answered with a grin. Jez had no idea what exactly Horace was planning, but she could tell he was serious about buying property and expanding his business holdings, so she nodded in agreement. "I have no doubt you will succeed. Just remember, you have friends on the water as well. If you need something that we can provide, let me know, because I will keep an eye out for you. I truly owe you for this favor, which is a great load off of my mind. Now I must take my leave, for I have other business to deal with tonight." They both set down their empty goblets and stood up.

"Indeed, I am sure you do, so I wish you well there and always." He offered his hand, and she shook it. "If you wouldn't mind too much though Jez, can you exit the back way, which goes through the kitchen? From the sound of things, the front salon is filling up and I should see to my guests for the evening. Most of them wish not to be discovered down here by anyone outside of their friends who also frequent our establishment, so it would be best if they did not see you seeing them..."

His voice dropped off, but Jez caught his meaning. Horace was actually being kind. For all Jez was dressed well enough, a pirate who also happened to be a colored person as well as a woman should not be seen in his high-class establishment.

"No problem," she replied as they parted company and he hurried off. At any other time, she would have been affronted by it, but Horace Manfred was not the prejudiced one, his clientele was. He was a good businessman though and someone she was glad to know, and he might prove useful if he was as ambitious as he claimed.

She slipped out back, winding her way through the now busy and overheated kitchen, dodging people hauling and preparing food, and then strode away in the gloom of evening, heading uptown to where Antonia's warehouse should be filled somewhat more impressively with the load she had brought in.

Once farther up on a rise in a clear spot, she took one last look down at the bay. She could make out *Revelation* with reefed sails, noting where her ship was anchored out in the bay again, and breathed a sigh of relief. Beppe had made sure to get them right out of the dock area then. Yet unless it was tied up at one of the smaller docks that was hidden in the curve of the hill below, there was still no sign of *Sea Witch*.

Walter was really going to get a piece of her mind over that!

CHAPTER THREE

enry Morgan may have been deemed the pirate king of Port Royal, but he was not universally loved by all. Besides Jacques Chagall, there were other men who envied Morgan yet hated him for his glib jests and cocky self-assurance while he was robbing fellow pirates of all their ill-gotten gains. Many of them had been decisively trounced by the portly Welshman in some business deal that often started with alcohol and gambling. Henry, even well into his cups, still paid close attention to what was being said or done around him. Now and then the outwardly affable Captain Morgan would make someone a casual offer of monetary assistance, though always with certain conditions attached because he was positive he would not be repaid on time. Everything was noted in official documents signed or at least verified before credible witnesses. Many of his peers could neither read nor write or even understand what he read to them, especially after a rather lengthy and complex explanation. Morgan always had some seemingly impartial observers nearby as he repeatedly asked the fellow if he understood what was being said. Most would simply swallow their pride and make their mark on the line indicated and then shake hands and go off wondering what half of that document actually meant. When the payment came due and it wasn't paid in full, then

Morgan would tack on so much compounding interest that whoever he was dealing with would have no choice but to lose their ship or business rather than go any deeper into debt. This did not make him any additional friends, but it did make him a wealthy and landed man.

Those type of ruthless business dealings, along with his intermittent raids on the settlements and treasure caravans of the Spanish Main, kept Morgan and his closest cronies in Port Royal living a very lavish existence.

When Walter Armitage woke up on *Danseuse* the next morning, he was quite hungover, but he had made up his mind what he intended to do. He was determined to worm his way into Morgan's inner circle. He knew full well that the man was a high-level flimflam artisan and that he was incredibly convincing. Yet Henry did protect his trusted friends quite ably and Walter wanted to become one of them. Walter was sick of his own dissolute hand-to-mouth existence of running down small local merchant ships and taking what little they had aboard, only to have it squandered away in a few boozy nights at anchor after a quick revel in some shabby port town.

Walter was also tired of risking his life so that someone else might prosper while he only got a cut of the before-sales allotment. As much as he had respected Émile Gagnon and wanted to help him and Antonia with their business, he hadn't wound up with much from working for them to call his own. To struggle away at sea day and night for only enough coin to restock the ship and have a quick frolicsome evening before heading back out again was not his idea of a good life. What he was seeing in Morgan's vision for Port Royal was what Tortuga had once promised. Pirates now ran the place, for they provided the protection that England refused to spend crown coin on.

He went up on deck and walked around. There was no one else aboard, for in Port Royal's harbor, nobody was going to steal your ship or cargo without incurring the wrath of Henry Morgan and being banned from coming back. Whatever might remain of Chagall's crew who hadn't left with Lévesque was likely ashore spending whatever coin they had or looking for a new berth on another vessel. He had the entire ship to himself.

He looked it over properly for the first time. While it was in decent shape, he decided he would take Morgan up on the offer to get the ship refitted to his own specifications. A fresh paint job for certain, for it needed careening anyway, and Port Royal did have a dry dock area available. A slightly different sail rig with properly apportioned canvas would help as well because she was carrying a lot of sail and that had to be tricky in storms or with making quick turns. Every captain had his preferences after all. Maybe a couple more cannons too. No noticeable leaks but there was battle damage in areas that had been patched. He'd see that all of it was permanently repaired before it got

When Walter Armitage woke up, he was quite hungover...

painted. And yes, that figurehead definitely had to go.

The ship also needed a new name. Whatever it would be rechristened needed to reflect what it was now meant to be, not what the former owner thought of it. *Danseuse* wasn't a bad name, since ships were always considered female and this one was as trim and lithe as a dancer, but it was too pretentious sounding for Walter's taste. While it wasn't one of the big and powerful looking vessels that would make those they pursued cringe in fear, he wanted his ship—the first one he had ever owned—to indicate cunning and speed rather than some delicately charming woman.

Ah, but women could be smart, tough, and tricky as well as winsome and alluring. All of them seemed to be vexing in one way or another. Jez certainly was a fine example of that combination of qualities. Well, he certainly wasn't naming his ship after her! Captain Johnston seemed to think rather highly of herself as it was. Still, she was certainly some inspiration.

Walter thought about it quite a bit as he wandered back down through the busy dock area, dodging men moving crates and barrels, sailors ambling into town to spend their pay, the usual dirty and ragged waterfront beggar waifs, and bawdy strumpets strolling about draped in satin and lace. He headed into the morning city, which was also bustling. For a fact, Port Royal never slept these days, that was something else you could thank Morgan and his pirate allies for.

After speaking with Henry the previous evening about it being an English port and having confessed his apprehension about being recognized as a wanted man, Walter felt a lot safer ashore here than in any other place he had harbored in. It really was Morgan's town, and Henry had proved to be a wise and shrewd member of the landed gentry as well as a successful pirate. He oft played the clown and was certainly a drunkard, but somehow he still always managed to come out on top. The man was as wily as a fox.

That last thought stopped Walter in his tracks. He and Henry Morgan were both originally lads from the English lands of Britain and Wales respectively, where sneaky foxes were the scourges of the big estates as well as the small farm cots. Walter's grandfather had been well enough off to have his own country manor where he owned horses and hounds for hunting such predator animals. As a young lad Walter recalled being envious, though the chases were long and hard on those involved, for they rode headlong all over the countryside, jumping their mounts over stone walls, hedges, and rills to follow the baying hounds. Now and then people were injured, and he'd seem some good horses lamed and a couple that had to be given the mercy killing, while meantime the fox, or whatever they sought, got away.

That had been a very long time ago, when Walter was newly into wearing knee breeches. He hadn't thought about it in years. He smiled, recalling no matter how regularly they raided the henhouses and rabbit warrens, as a boy he had always cheered for those sleek and sly ruddy-coated creatures to escape. He tried to recall, what was the female of the fox species called now...?

It finally came to him. A vixen. Vixen was a grand title for a modest sized but fleet ship that could take on larger vessels and yet slip away quickly when chased. *Vixen* she would be called, and someday he'd have a figurehead to match it.

Walter now had a name for his new ship. In spite of his throbbing hangover that morning, his pace picked up a jaunty aspect as he went forth to seek out Morgan once more and take him up on his offer. If Henry could get the ship—*Vixen*—refitted and ready to sail at a reasonable fee, he'd give him whatever was left aboard from the raid with Jez.

He also had to find Jean-Claude and have him start rounding up whoever was left of their crew that were willing to re-sign with him so they could move *Vixen* over to the dry dock area. For the first time in a couple of years Walter felt as if he had some hope of a decent future. He cast aside all thoughts of Jez and Antonia then and focused on getting his new vessel ready to sail by whatever means he could. His burgeoning friendship with Henry Morgan was going to turn his life around for the better.

Perhaps someday he too would own land and businesses on Jamaica. Then he'd have more ships under his command. Once he was established, he could find himself a proper wife and have some children while he was still young enough to enjoy them, for a man with such holdings needed to produce some heirs to inherit them and run the place once he retired to writing his memoirs. No more drunken nights after wasted days sailing around aimlessly after random prizes. Ah, things looked so much cheerier now!

Walter found Jean-Claude in a tavern talking to a couple of other pirates he'd been drinking with for hours. They were celebrating something and were about to head out to one of the brothels.

"Ah, Walter mon ami, come join us!" his quartermaster said in a jovial tone, though those with him appeared guarded at best.

"I would prefer to speak with you alone first Jean-Claude," Walter began but the man waved him off.

"Later mon frère, we have women waiting for us. Young and healthy ones with nice soft pink skin on their plump arms, firm seins," he spread his open hands on his chest and then patted his own behind, "and round derrières a man can squeeze. No pox, no clap! And all free!"

"Really now?" Walter stood with his arms crossed on his chest, tapping a foot impatiently. "Since when did you become so wealthy my friend?" What Jean-Claude had described sounded like one of the newer, more upscale brothels. There was no way these men could afford that!

"Since I signed on with Captain Morgan as sous-lieutenant on one of his better ships. Everyone who signs on gets a bonus like that in port. We chose ours today."

That did not please Walter at all. "I just bought us a new and bigger ship and so I assumed that you would have been quartermaster of that as well. Why would you take a demotion to serve with Morgan?"

"Très simple! He will pay me better than you have," Jean-Claude said glibly, but then he noticed the scowl on his now former captain's face. "Plus, I can advance with him, peut-être become capitaine someday. You got a good ship now, you can go find someone else younger and more patient than moi. I want to make a lot of money, Walter, so I can have plenty more fun, *tu vois?* I'm too old to keep living on these little handouts."

He started to lurch away but Walter grabbed his shoulder yanked him back. "So just *when* were you planning on telling me this?" Jean-Claude gave him a quick scowl, but then he laughed and shrugged.

"You know now. *So bon chance mon ami,* and don't forget, this is the pirate life after all. Every man for himself, eh?" With a big grin showing one tooth of old gold and a few missing teeth, Jean-Claude pulled away and staggered off.

A disgusted Walter let him go whoring with his new friends, cussing them out under his breath for ruining his formerly jubilant mood. He sat down heavily at their vacated table, ordering himself some ale and food. He ate in silence as he thought things over. He didn't feel very much like speaking to Morgan just yet. He wasn't happy that the man was stealing his crew out from under him.

At least Pakke should still remain loyal. They had been together a long time. He hadn't seen the young Panamanian native since he came ashore to find Henry Morgan. Walter wondered what Pakke had been up to all this time, for Morgan had told him when his men had come to get *Sea Witch*, it was all but abandoned.

At least that was Henry's story. Walter wasn't sure what he should believe anymore.

He ordered one more ale and then forced himself to drink up and leave so that he remained sober. Surely there had to be other good men in this town who would sign with him! He'd have to start haunting the waterfront taverns or inexpensive inns with taprooms, looking for those who had yet to make their X with someone, but he was determined to have a few choice words with Morgan as well.

Once finished he paid for his meal and drinks and left a coin tip on the table for the serving wench and then wandered out in the midday sun. He should initially see if any of his original crew would rejoin, though almost all of them spoke French and very little English. Without Jean-Claude to translate for him it would be a rough first outing. This couldn't have come at a worst time!

Bah, it's an English colony, I'll find men I can use, he told himself as he left the tavern. *If Jez can find a crew that works hard for her, so can I!* He walked parallel to the harbor, lost in his thoughts, gazing at all the ships. There were certainly enough of them out there. Some of them must have men who could be lured away with promises of working for the man who had purchased old Jacques Chagall's trim vessel.

Walter had stopped at a rise in the road to study his new ship from afar, wondering what color to repaint her. Ruddy brown with black trim and white sails would look fine. Realizing he was stalling before confronting Morgan for luring away his crew, he turned to go look for Henry and almost collided with someone else.

"Sorry, I guess I was woolgathering," Walter said with a shrug to a tall and far younger man who was scowling at him. In silent answer that man rammed a fist into his stomach. The lightning quick punch to the gut caught him completely by surprise. Walter doubled over in pain and almost retched up his meal.

"Chagall says bonjour!" the man who had hit him snarled; his voice full of rancor fueled by the very noticeable fumes of rum.

He had punched pretty hard, and it hurt like hell, yet it could have been a knife instead. Walter forced himself upright, still gagging and reeling, and he said in a croak to the man who was staggering off, "Thank you for not killing me outright."

"That too could be arranged," his assailant snapped with a thick French accent, though his English was quite good. He stopped and turned enough to glare back at Walter, weaving just a bit from the drink.

"You are a friend of old one-eyed Jock?" Walter asked him and the man glowered even more.

"I am—or I was—a shipmate, but no more now that Morgan who stole our ship has sold it to you, Anglais. Capitaine Chagall is in bad shape from his duel with Morgan and because of that I have nowhere else to go."

Walter scoffed at that. "I was there when it happened, and it was no duel. They were playing cards and Morgan won. Jock accused Morgan of cheating and pulled a pistol on him, but Henry fired first."

"Under the table! That is a coward's way!" the other man snarled, his face livid with anger.

"It was him or Chagall, we all saw that. Morgan could have killed Jock but he didn't." The man staggered back toward Walter and shook a fist in his face.

"Morgan crippled him on purpose to make him even more ashamed for not being willing to join one of his big ambitious raids! Now we have no ship, no crew, and no one will sign me on. All because I spoke out and defended my capitaine against a dirty dealing Welshman who thinks he owns the entire island and everyone on it. I am a man of honor who stands behind his capitaine, so I had my say, even though all his bootlicking lapdogs warned me that here in Port Royal, Morgan is the law." He sneered at that. "And that fat son of a pig-fucking whore just laughed at me and then had his lackeys throw me out into the filthy gutter. So, this has cost me much too, as I now have a bad reputation here. Maybe I should call you out as well and win our ship back—eh?"

For all the man's drink-fueled anger made him dangerous, Walter could almost sympathize with him. Henry Morgan could be overbearing, ruthless, and cold-blooded, and he certainly held a lot of sway with the other pirates in this port. The man who had attacked him was both furious and desperate, for he had doubled his fists and was now dancing around Walter. At least he wasn't armed with a blade.

"You don't want to do this," Walter said, as he put up his own fists in a guard position and began to take a fighting stance, noting that people were starting to look their way. A quick left jab to his right ear that snapped his head sideways said otherwise. This one was quick on his feet and if he had been sober, he'd be a lot less clumsy.

"Oh, but certainment I do," the other man said with exaggerated conviction. The next punch thrown was a left uppercut that hit Walter squarely on the chin, though because he saw it coming, he managed to pull back. It had a little power behind it; this trim fellow could really mess you up if he wanted to. The young man was fast, and he knew how to fight, but he was drunk enough that he was sloppy with his timing. He was about Walter's height but more slightly built so he had some speed. He followed up with a fast right uppercut that missed and then he ducked out as Walter came back at him with a flurry of alternating crosses, trying to back him up and maybe take him off his feet in an attempt to end it quickly.

Walter was a realist, he already knew his opponent could beat him if it went on too long. The man was younger and faster moving as well as angry enough at the world to be dangerous. Even while drunk he fought well enough to wary of, because a lucky punch could end it at any time. The younger man was grinning now, for he was keeping Walter on his toes, trying to wear the older man out. Most pirates fought with blades which added some distance, but neither of them was wearing a hanger at the moment and Walter wasn't about to pull a knife. This did not feel like a serious battle anyway, it seemed more like a test of sorts.

Fine, he'd show the lad what a soldier turned freebooter learns about close quarters encounters when your fists and your wits were all you had at your disposal.

He began to lunge in at the stranger, taking a few hits, one which bloodied his lower lip and another that landed on the breastbone and nearly knocked the wind from him again. Yet Walter also gave as good as he got, pummeling away with brutal combinations that had far more precision. That kept his opponent continually backing off. Walter was no youngster, and he was clearly out of shape, for he hadn't been doing all that much fighting lately. Most of their boardings of prize ships from *Sea Witch* had been relatively peaceable with minimal resistance from the crews of the vessels they had overtaken. That and all the excessive drinking had put him and the crew in a more dissipated state. He was breathless and gasping as they fought, but he was relatively sober and let instinct take over where speed and agility failed him.

They were drawing quite a crowd now, some of them cheering and jeering, many placing bets.

Chagall's man was pretty good at guarding his upper body, and he still moved fast. Walter was tiring quickly after waking hungover, so if this went on too long, he would make a costly mistake. He changed tactics and coming in low, did manage to get in a couple of pretty hard blows to the stomach, which while rock hard on the younger man, was still full of alcohol and someone's stew and bread. The man reeled and Walter thought he had him, but then the desperate youngster came back with a wild haymaker of a punch that missed completely and set him off-balance. He collapsed into Walter's arms instead, and his face went pale before he spewed everything he had recently eaten and drank all over the both of them before his stunned opponent could shove him away. The younger man landed on his rear in the dust of the road.

"Ye gods, what a sneaky way to end a damn fight!" Walter complained with disgust, for the relatively clean shirt he had put on that morning was now heavily soiled with the partially digested contents of his opposition's last meal. Besides them both being sweat soaked, they now smelled like a couple of drunken babies in two-day-old diaper cloths.

The gathered crowd was roaring in laughter. Nobody was getting rich on this one, so most of them good-naturedly dispersed to go drink and talk about the fight that ended in a rather unusual conclusion.

"It was not my intention to do so, of course," the other man replied in a hoarse croak as he looked down at his own soiled clothing. "And this my best port outfit!" It sounded so pitifully girlish that Walter also had to laugh.

"Not so nice anymore, is it?" He strode forward and offered his younger adversary a hand up. "I'll call this a draw if you promise not to puke on me again. I think we'd better find a horse trough somewhere and get cleaned up and then maybe we can talk about your current lack of employment."

The other man gave him a strange look as he came back up to his feet. "You would have me aboard your ship after I fought with you?"

Walter shrugged. "Well, you proved you have fidelity to your captain and crew as well as plenty of nerve, so I figure it might be safer to have you on my side. I am Captain Walter Armitage. What's your name lad?"

"Arnaud, and that is all you need to know about me," the young man said rather primly for someone covered in smelly dark slime. They still had a small crowd of curious onlookers who followed the two men tramping aimlessly together until they found a well where an older woman was drawing water. They waited patiently at a short distance until she was finished and then drew several buckets for themselves, sluicing each other down. They didn't talk to one another because there was little left to say at the moment. It was an uneasy silence.

"I guess this is as clean as we will get out here," a dripping wet Walter finally said after looking down at his own clothing and then at the man who was standing next to him, still swaying a bit on his feet. This one being fairly young was not such a bad thing, for youthful energy was a boon on board. He cautiously stepped closer and asked in a low voice, "What position did you hold on Chagall's ship?"

Arnaud gave him a frown. "I was his last quartermaster. I replaced the previous man who had trained me as a mate when he got killed a year or so ago. Chagall trusted him and because of that he trusted me enough to offer the promotion. Thankfully, the crew agreed. What does it matter to you Anglais? You have our ship; do you plan to mock me as well? Perhaps make me a common sailor again? Maybe you are just looking for another fight?" His fists had come up again as he stepped closer.

"No, no more fighting between us." Walter pushed those fists down. "However, I might consider hiring you on as my own quartermaster, since Morgan just signed mine out from under me to one of his own ships. Would you be interested in that position?"

"Why did you not ask sooner?" Arnaud said. "I might still have a belly full of stew and dry clothing!"

"Arnaud, you never gave me a chance. Next time, maybe talk to someone who might hire you before you walk up and punch him in the gut."

"Fine, so this has not been my best day. I admit that! But I have lost everything I had in the world; do you understand that Anglais? I have nowhere to go but on the streets, begging once more." His voice was low and somber, and Walter could hear true anguish in it.

"Then come with me, and we will fix that right off." They began to walk down to the docks together. "I have clean clothing aboard—all my things were moved there, for your captain's belongings were moved out and it appears the crew took theirs too. Some of it should fit you, we are about the same height."

"I am the one who took Chagall his belongings, and I never made it back in time to secure my own. Likely then the crew took mine as well, so I have nothing but what I wear now," Arnaud said with chagrin. "Even my last coin is gone, for other than the meal, I gave what I had toward my Capitaine's care."

Walter was actually impressed by that; this man was a cut above the average pirate. He seemed to have been educated at some point too. "You're welcome to check aboard for your belongings, but I too suspect they are likely history by now. There was no drink left behind either so someone got that."

They both sighed. Raiding a sold ship was a pirate thing. Walter continued explaining what they were up against.

"Look Arnaud, I am unsure how much if any of my crew will be coming back at this point, because Morgan and his cronies have been signing as many able-bodied men as they can get," he added as he cut across the narrow strip of beach to the boardwalk and then headed for the dock where his new ship—*Vixen* he reminded himself—was tied up. "Yet at least your crew has left me all that I owned and didn't rob the necessary ship's stores. I saw it all aboard below, though some of it is poorly stowed because they were hunting for the rum. Plus, they left everything on the orlop deck, and they didn't strip her magazine of shot or powder."

"Those are things to be thankful for. Men can be replaced here, but ship stores are too expensive," Arnaud said as they walked the length of the dock and then climbed aboard the ship one at a time. "You will refit her before we sail, I assume?"

Walter nodded. "I have to. For one thing she needs a careening and repaint, and I prefer to get it all done at once while we have a decent dry dock. I made a deal with Morgan to do so while we were out celebrating, and he was in somewhat of a generous mood. Still, he wants the rest of my cargo that was aboard my last ship, now that the men are paid off."

"That island sloop you came in on? She could not hold too much with such a large crew aboard."

Walter grinned; Arnaud got points for being observant. They had gained the weather deck, scrambling over the gunnel between lines and were standing together, looking around. "Normally I'd agree with you, but we hit a worthwhile prize, a leaky old caravel filled with wealthy Portuguese pilgrims sailing home with all their worldly goods." The man's eyes lit up as he turned his gaze on his new captain. "I had a partner with a small brig, and they loaded the bigger items like furniture and household stuff to take back to Tortuga where there is a shop run by a mutual friend. I made sure we got all the coins, jewelry, small porcelain, and some church pieces that were gilt or silver—all easy for us to stow aboard and they sell or trade rather high. I had planned on trading up for a bigger vessel. That's why I came here, and what I was seeing Morgan about."

"That was wise of you," Arnaud said with admiration in his voice as he looked around the ship he had served on for several years, not expecting to be back aboard after all that had happened over the last few days. "You know Walter, I did not expect to be standing on this deck again, not with Chagall crippled like he is. He tells me he will heal in time, they say to me that even if the black rot does not set in, he will never walk without a crutch. Jacques loved this ship, it was like a loyal and beautiful woman who always embraced him with welcoming arms, so he will grow old and feeble fast without her. Yet I suppose this had to happen someday, he took too many chances, and he was no young man anymore."

Arnaud's voice dropped off and he sighed, but then he asked," Tell me though, what will become of the dancer?" He indicated the figurehead and seemed a bit uneasy about it.

Walter rubbed his stubbly chin on that. This was an opportunity to see how well they would work together. "What would you suggest?"

There was no hesitation. "Remove it first and give it back to Chagall, for he prized it above all else. I believe there was once a woman he coveted whose likeness he had carved into it. He stays in a place where they take good care of him, and there is a shed in the back. Wrapped in old canvas, it should be safe. Give him the nameplate too. He paid dearly for both, all that gold leaf had to be renewed each year. Perhaps he can open a tavern or something and use it for a sign."

That was actually a brilliant solution and well thought out. Walter was again impressed—Arnaud had good insight on what motivated people. Walter had thought of selling the figurehead, but this was something he could do to win this wise young pirate over.

"I will certainly do that, but I want you to present it to him because it was your idea. Besides he will not want to see me, and I have enough enemies right now as it is," Walter said with a half-laugh. In truth, he no longer knew who to trust.

"Gladly will I offer him that much comfort, for all he trusted me. You will rename the ship of course. Do you have any idea what to call it?"

That Walter was eager to answer, though he had to be careful how much he said about how and why. They were now headed toward the stern. "I have at least come up with that much. She will be called *Vixen*, though I cannot afford another figurehead right now." He got a confused look.

"That is a name I do not know," Arnaud told him as they went down the ladder to the captain's cabin.

"It's what we English call a female fox," Walter said as he began going through his sea chest, which along with a canvas bag of other small items from *Sea Witch*'s captain's cabin had been deposited somewhat in the way. He looked up a moment when he didn't get an immediate reply. "You do have foxes in France I am told." He did not care to admit he had fought there against the French; it was too soon for that revelation.

"Yes, but I lived in the city, so I have never seen one. We call them renard for the male, and renarde is the female." The difference in pronunciation was so subtle that Walter couldn't pick it out.

"In England the male is a dog fox. It's easier to have a name that is distinct to the ear." He tossed Arnaud some clean clothes.

"No doubt for the Anglais that would be necessary," the other man said as he stripped and began to re-dress. He would need a belt or sash. Walter's waist was larger so the breeches would not stay up. "But why that name? What does it mean to you?" he continued as they both were changing, piling the soiled clothing in a heap.

"This ship," Walter said, "is like a fox: it can run fast, it can turn sharply, and it can be devious in outwitting pursuers. I have seen foxes do that, and none of them are more tricksome than the females, for they often have pups to protect. Plus, it is what we call a woman who schemes to have things her way, by lying, artifice, or other means. So, I decided that *Vixen* would make a good name for her."

"Ah yes, *cherchez la femme* as we say; it means that when there is trouble afoot, to look for the woman behind it." Arnaud sighed wistfully and Walter himself could relate, so he decided there must be a story behind that reaction. Again, that would come with trust in time.

"*Vixen* is a name that was well thought out then," Arnaud admitted as he tied his breeches up with a sash that Walter offered him. It was something fancy, a length of bronze satin that ended in tassels.

"Thanks. You can keep that sash. I never liked it. I looked like a walking curtain in it."

Arnaud laughed. "As long as it keeps my pantalon in place, I will not complain too much. You have been most generous with a man who tried to beat you to death."

"Beggars can't be choosers I suppose," Walter said with a shrug. "I do need an experienced quartermaster who knows the ship, is not afraid to fight, and can keep men in line. Now let us go find somewhere to eat where the food is good, the serving wenches are comely, and the rum worth lingering for. I still need to speak with Morgan at some point, but that can wait. Right now we need to figure out who we can trust signing on as crew so we can get this ship in shape."

CHAPTER FOUR

Jez made it to the warehouse shop of Antonia Campos just in time to see it being closed for the day. They had certainly worked late. A weary Jobah had been watering the team with a bucket before they hauled the wagon back to Antonia's carriage house. He had just taken his normal seat up front when she showed up.

"Miz Jez," he said politely, tipping his worn out hat. "We be done here for the day and all locked up. The fellas told me the ladies headed back to the house whilst I was bringing the last load up, so we took the time to get it all inside and then they put my seat back lower so's I can get it into the carriage house without knocking meself out. You be wantin' a ride back to the house I s'pose?"

"That would be greatly appreciated Jobah, it's been a long day," she said. Jez hadn't really spoken to Jobah much before, but noticed his phrasing had very little French influence. That was becoming more common on Tortuga with the influx of English settlers starting plantations. Perhaps he'd been a slave on one of them?

"It surely was a long one, but a good day at that." He moved over to make room for her, and taking the reins with one hand, offered a hand up. Jez plopped down beside him, and he slapped the reins before turning the tired draft team to go back up the road one last time. "These old fellas gonna be glad to get inta that stall t'night," he commented. "I got one of yer mam's boys as likes te help wit' the unharnessing and so on. Standing on a keg he'll give them a good rubdown. No worries, he'll be safe. They be good ol hosses, nice and quiet if'n a bit lazy at times."

"Glad to hear that. You go ahead and put those boys to work, they need to learn some responsibilities. Plus it keeps them out of trouble. We're all lucky that Antonia has been generous in bringing my family up here."

"She's a fine and gentle spoken lady for one born to them Spanish royals." Obviously Hetty was doing her share of gossiping about their employer.

"I think Mister Émilien had a lot to do with teaching her how to handle herself here on Tortuga," Jez said, using Antonia's late beau's assumed surname on Tortuga.

"No doubt there! Now that one, he was a good man; always friendly and respectful to one and all. We sure do miss him."

"Yes, we do Jobah, all of us do," Jez said with feeling as she sat back with her arms crossed over her chest. Émile Gagnon was sorely missed, for he had been easy going and yet he knew how to handle people. Gagnon was unsuited to be a pirate, for he detested the excitement of eminent danger and all the bloodshed involved. That he managed to successfully escape that life but then died violently ashore anyway was a travesty. A solemn but amiable silence passed between Jez and Jobah as thoughts of what had been and how things were now occupied both minds.

The team was tired and Jobah wasn't pushing them. Their soft clopping in the warm and humid evening air was making Jez drowsy. To keep from nodding off she studied the buildings around her as they slowly changed from typical crowded two-story city architecture, most with ground floor shops and rooms for living quarters in the level above, to the wealthier merchant homes that studded the area where Antonia lived. She yawned and stretched as Jobah turned the team into Antonia's road.

"Almost there now Miz Jez," he remarked as they drove down the curving lane and drew in sight of the house and garden. "Hey now—that be Doc Burden's carriage out front! I sure hope nobody got sick or hurt!"

That wasn't a good sign. "Let me off here Jobah!" Jez insisted as he swung the horses in toward the far side cart track that would take him to the stable building well out back. Jobah called, "Whoa!" and sawed on the reins but before the wagon came to a full stop Jez had already vaulted over the side and was racing through the front garden to get to the door. She pounded on that and a weeping and shaking Marie-Louise opened it.

"What happened?" Jez insisted

"Oh Miz Jez, it be awful," the girl said in the most dramatic tone. "Mistress Antonia, she... she... She been shot!"

Jez shoved-armed the girl aside and rushed past her, banging through the inner doorway when she heard loud voices raised in accusatory anger. One of them was her mother, and Monifa was almost screaming. That was enough for Jez, who yanked free her hanger and barged in to a room filled with a howling baby, yelling adults, and furniture in utter chaos. There was a puddle of blood on the floor, but it was not from Antonia, who sat slumped on the settee but

"We're all lucky that Antonia has been generous in bringing my family up here."

appeared only minimally injured. She was pale as a fresh sailcloth though and a pistol lay next to her. She seemed to have been nicked in the shoulder by something. Having just carefully eased her arm out of the torn and blood spotted sleeve of her dress, Old Doctor Burden stooped over her.

"It's not too bad, barely more than a scratch," he told Antonia in a soft and comforting voice as he finished winding a bandage up and over it. "I can give you something for the pain." Only then did he look up and see Jez. "Captain Johnston, I presume?" he asked with a slight frown.

"Yes. What happened here?" Jez said, sheathing her sword. She sidestepped the blood and came to Antonia's side.

"Well, the way I heard it, there was an attempted robbery involved, and somebody shot the man who was trying to burglarize this house. His gun went off and hit Miss Antonia."

"Where is he?" Jez snapped with a scowl, her hand back on her sword's hilt.

"Long gone," the doctor said with an arch look. "Leastwise, he was when I got here. So, you can leave that pig sticker put away please, we've had enough bloodshed for one day." After handing Antonia a small bottle with a dropper and warning her to keep it well out of reach of the children, he began packing up to leave before he headed back to the front entry. Jez waited until Marie-Louise let him out the door before she spoke.

"I'll find the bastard, he won't get far with that much blood loss," she said, but her mother gave her a warning shake of her head. Antonia grabbed for her as well.

"Jez, please don't get involved, this is bad enough already," Antonia whispered as she sat up and handed off the pistol to her. Jez checked it; it had been recently fired.

"What the hell happened?" Jez said in frustration, plopping down on the couch next to Antonia, who was sitting upright now, running a long-fingered hand over her face. Now that the doctor had left, Monifa sat down in a chair nearby, rocking a fretful Camille while Davey huddled at her side. They were watching Hetty and Marie-Louise mopping up the blood on the floor with old rags.

"We got word from the boys—your brothers—that a man was watching the house. They had been in the barn, cleaning out the muck."

"I tole dem to do that," Monifa interrupted. "They must earn their keep."

"Go on," Jez prompted Antonia after giving her mother a quick nod.

"One of them ran down to notify us, the other stayed behind to keep watch. We had Davey with us at the warehouse to help watch the baby while we were busy sorting and writing things down. I did not like hearing that, so I told the men that when Jobah came back with the final load they should finish bringing everything inside and close up. We four caught a ride with someone and came right back home; unfortunately, we had to walk part of the way to get here. When I came in the yard, I could see that the front door was open and I found Hetty and Marie-Louise hiding in the garden shed. They said the man threatened them and he had a pistol. We left the little ones with them. So I went in the back way, while your mother... she went in the servant's entrance. A man was going through my things in here, he was tossing them around, looking for something. He did have a pistol, but not this one, it is mine—it was Émile's, but he kept it loaded and taught me a little about how to point and shoot. I told Monifa just to get it for me, but the man had pointed his own gun at me, and there was no time..."

Jez had a sick feeling in her stomach. She turned to her mother.

"*You* shot him?" She got a defiant yes nod. "Was he hurt bad?"

"Bad enough," Monifa said in a low tone. "Your Papa showed me how to aim a gun some good many years ago. That's why I always kept a pistol in the tavern. You know all that Jez. Being alone at cashing out time is always dangerous."

"What did you do—fire right past Antonia and hit her?"

"No, I am not that stupide!" Monifa said in a huff.

Antonia broke in. "His gun went off when she shot him and I did not move fast enough. Thankfully the shot only nicked me though it scared Marie-Louise out of her wits."

Jez sighed in relief. "So, if the doctor only saw Antonia with a pistol, all he knows is somebody shot a robber. Well, this is her house, so that is her right. They should take your word for what happened over that of a thief."

"I do not think so Jez," Antonia said bleakly. "This man was not a common thief; he was much more well dressed. Also, he said, 'If that nigger you are living with does not put the gun down, I will see that the governor has her hanged and her four bastard brats are all sold on the block.' We did not have the children inside but he knew all about who lives here."

Jez turned to face her mother again. "So that's when you shot him? *After* he warned you what would happen?" she said with incredulity in her voice. Monifa bridled at that.

"Yes! I am a free woman Jez, I have papers your Papa signed. Everyone knows that! My children are all freeborn too. Nobody threatens my family and gets away with it while I still live. Miz Antonia took the gun from me after he run off and then we bring the others inside. We sent D'Jimy down for the doctor. Miz Antonia tole that doctor she shot the man who was here. So, all is good."

"No, it is *not* all good," Jez snapped. "This is an ugly mess!" She held her head in her hands. A negro attacking a white man ashore, even if he was breaking in to steal something from the household the colored person lived in, was likely to result in jail time. Even touching a gun, let along shooting someone, would be a capital offense. If the man survived long enough to talk, Monifa would hang, for everyone would believe the story of a white man over anything a woman or someone colored said.

"I need to find him, which way did he go?" Jez said, getting to her feet. Antonia was crying with her hands over her face, and she couldn't get a coherent word out. So Monifa answered.

"He be gut shot, he won't get far. Your Papa always said aim for the center 'cause is biggest part. Just follow the blood."

Just like that, it became Jez's problem. Well that's how it usually was for Jezebel Johnston, who too often had to fix everyone else's predicaments.

It was getting dark out, but fortunately there were plenty of blood splashes to follow. Whoever the man was, thankfully he did not get far for he never even made it out of the yard. He had curled into a ball and died beneath a sprawling gumbo-limbo tree, the drooping branches quite effectively hiding his body. Jez was tall enough that she had to duck down underneath the big widespread branches to actually spot him.

He was beginning to stiffen but she managed to turn him over somewhat, enough to get a decent look at him. She was surprised he was such a young man, just barely out of his teen years. Her mother was right, he was definitely gut shot, rather low and at that short range it had torn through his vitals. He had bled out profusely.

This was no nobleman though; for all he was well dressed, the clothing was mismatched, worn thin, and did not fit well. She bent closer and noted there was still some tar in his closely cropped light blond hair. His hands had been scrubbed clean, but his nails were ragged and tar stained too. He had a healed scar on his chin from a blade cut and with his teeth gritted and lips drawn back in a grimace of pain; she noted the signs of scurvy. A sailor then, likely a pirate. Someone else would definitely have sent him to rummage through the house.

Which also meant he would have been expected to report back. Someone would notice he was missing.

Jez was a pirate; she had robbed dead men before. She spotted the pistol next to him and carefully picked it up. It was a very nice piece with a lot of engraving on the metal and a steel tipped wooden rammer in good condition, so well worth having. Making sure it wasn't cocked; she tucked that into her sash. There was something stuffed into his shirt, so Jez gingerly reached inside and found a leather pouch that had the crunch of coin within. She wasn't sure if that was his pay or something from Antonia's house, so took that as well. She backed out from underneath the gumbo-limbo and stood up, quickly shoving the pouch inside her own shirt front, hoping it wasn't all sticky with drying blood.

The dead burglar could remain there for now while Jez worked out how to get him out of Antonia's yard unseen once it was nighttime No doubt the doctor would send someone up in the morning to inquire about what had happened. Jez did not want anyone finding his body, for he was still well enough dressed to be missed. Let whoever sent him think he absconded with the coin he was paid—likely the pistol as well. She would have to go through his clothing more thoroughly once she had him somewhere safer to do so. They couldn't bury him on the island, the soil was rocky and full of roots, and freshly turned earth was a dead giveaway to the curious that something had been dug out or buried there. On an island with a pirate port, that could be well worth digging up again. The best place to hide a body would be out at sea, but they weren't ready to sail yet.

Maybe Jobah would have an idea how to get him quietly down to the harbor. She'd need the elder man's help getting this one out of the yard anyway. Jez headed back inside to speak to Antonia and her mother, and then she'd have to talk to Jobah privately about moving the body. This was not something Hetty, or especially Marie-Louise, could be involved in. They both loved to gossip.

When Jez came inside, her mother was feeding the children in the dining area. She looked up at Jez hovering in the doorway and noted the frown. "You are back so soon. Did you not find him?"

"We will discuss this later," Jez told her in that tone that meant, 'not in front of the little ones'. "Where is Antonia?"

"Oh, she need to rest. She go upstairs."

Jez nodded and then smiling at the children, headed up to where Antonia was sitting alone at her little table with a half-filled glass of wine. She was staring out the window at nothing, for it was getting dark, though a small candle in a holder on the little cabinet where things were stored softly illuminated the interior.

"May I come in?" Jez asked in a low tone, and Antonia jumped convulsively, almost upsetting the wine.

"Please do," she said in a breathless tone. "And shut the door. There is a bottle and glasses on the sideboard."

Closing the door silently behind her, Jez came over and after pouring herself a glass, sat across from Antonia. "I didn't mean to startle you, I just needed to let you know that I found him. He is still in the back yard." At the other woman's wary but inquiring look Jez nodded. "He is quite dead."

"Oh Jez," Antonia said with a half-sob as she put her hands up to her face. "I may go to hell for saying it, but that is some relief. Yet what can we do now? We will have to report it, and when they come to get him, they will question us. And your mother—always she says too much!"

"We can't let any of that happen," Jez said firmly. "I'll speak with Jobah. I believe he will hold his tongue. He and I can get the body out of here by first light. I wish I had the crewboat because I'd row him out to *Revelation* tonight, but that is just not going to happen. We can wind him in old canvas and tie some ballast rocks to it and drop him overboard out at sea once we leave." Antonia looked shocked at that, but Jez just shrugged. "It's how we bury men who have died while we're too far from land and it's more than that fiend deserved."

"Did you know him?" Antonia asked in an earnest tone, and Jez shrugged.

"I don't believe so, he was no one I recognized. He didn't appear to be dressed all that well, most of what he wore was just cast-off clothing or the kind of things the crew takes in pirate raids. It was getting dark out and his front was covered in dried blood, but I could tell he was a sailor recently. He's definitely been on shipboard, there was still tar in his hair and some showing black under his fingernails, and he's had a bit of scurvy. So, he was most likely hired by someone else to break in here and look for something they wanted. I would guess he'd been a pirate because he had to be fairly bold to just walk in and start going through your stuff. Plus, he had an old scar on his chin.

"Oh, and if this isn't yours, somebody did pay him." She fished the pouch out of her shirt and thumped it down on the table. It was lightly spattered with blood and Antonia recoiled and retched, covering her mouth and looking away. She waved a thin fingered hand at Jez

"No, that is not mine. Now please... take it away! I do not want it in my house!"

Jez tucked it back where she had it before. "Fine. So, you won't want his pistol either."

"No, I do not!" Antonia snapped with her voice rising in a high pitch. She was beginning to sound hysterical. "You can keep whatever he has with him unless you know it belongs to me. Just please Jez, get him off my property."

"All right," Jez said, getting to her feet. "You get some rest. I'll go talk to Jobah."

Jobah had already eaten his dinner and undressed down to a rather sweaty smock when Jez came for him. He, Hetty, and Marie-Louise shared the

cramped servant's quarters in a small cabin out back, just off the kitchen. He had obviously been filled in by the two women about the day's events for when Jez told him they had to speak outside, he just nodded sagely and asked her to meet him in the stable.

Antonia's loyal but aged dark skinned freedman was there just a few minutes later, dressed in the clothing he had worn that day. "I tole them two windbags to stay put and mind the house," Jobah said as he shut the stable door behind him. He had brought a candle stub with him and carefully lit a lantern with it, and then blew the stub out, for there was hay and bedding everywhere. "What you be needin' from me Miz Jez?" he asked her.

"I am so sorry to bother you after such a long day Jobah, but we have a big problem here that I need your help with. You heard about what happened today?"

"All blessed evenin'. I warned them two cheepin' biddies, you can't be talkin' 'bout this outside the house or in front of the chillun, 'cause if it gets out, somebody is gonna swing for it. They knows how us colored folks git the blame for ever'thin'. I take it we have somethin' needs doin' after dark?"

She nodded. "Unfortunately, yes. I found the body of the man who was shot. He's dead. He's also white and somebody paid him well." Jobah sucked in a breath at that and ran a hand through his thin gray hair. "The pistol he had on him was a nice piece too, so he likely got that from someone with some coin to his name. I think he might have been a pirate—I can tell he's seen ship time. Right now we need to get him out of Tortuga and fast, before someone comes looking on the morrow. I can't carry him by myself."

Jobah stroked his stubbly chin. "Well, that's a bit of a problem see, 'cause whilst I got a handcart we can use and I know my way through these woods, it ain't easy diggin' in this blasted rocky soil. Maybe we can jist dump him somewheres?"

Jez shook her head. "No, I wouldn't do that. If I can find a way to get him down to the harbor and into a small boat, I'll row him out to my ship, and we'll deal with making him disappear once we're at sea. Problem is, we're not ready to sail just yet, I have to resupply and my crew is taking turns at coming ashore. But at least if we get him stowed aboard that will end the search."

"That could be done, but we're gonna look awful funny trundlin' somethin' down to the harbor at night. We got guards in the city now that like to stop us colored folks and nose about in what we be doin'."

There was always something! Jez sighed unhappily. Then Jobah had an idea.

"What say we be taking a big ole barrel load of salt fish down to yer ship? We got us a partial one in the warehouse someone traded to Mister Émilien fer an item the man wanted awful bad, and the Mister was a soft touch so's he took it. Been nobody eatin' much o' it but me and the missus 'cause white folks be awful fussy—even though ma Hetty kin fix it right tasty. I can bring that up now, and we'll just bundle him up good and tight down inside and then dump some of them fish atop. Ain't nobody gonna paw through all that stink. We gotta work fast though, 'cause it takes time to load it and then unload it."

"What if we do get stopped though?" Jez asked. "Won't it be kind of obvious trundling something like that around at night?"

"Hell Miz Jez, it's gonna be mid-mawnin' by the time we get down as far as the docks. You tell 'im you's got hungry men aboard is all. And if that don' satisfy them, well... we'll jist make somethin' else up!" was Jobah's answer.

It was all they had, so Jez shrugged and said, "I guess we have to use whatever we've got. My only other concern is there's a lot of blood out back. That'll draw flies and anybody who knows about wounded or dead men will look for it. They might even have dogs."

"So, we best go git that man and bring him inside, and then go fetch that barrel right off and get him loaded init," Jobah said with a yawn. "As fer as gettin' it down to the docks, ye'll have ta handle the rest, 'cause I got work fer me up here. I got a nice big smelly pile o' manure and beddin' right out back this stable I can use to cover up any mess that fella done made. One nose fulla that and no dog is gonna smell anythin' else fer a while. We'd best skedaddle though 'cause it's gonna take some time to pull this all together and then I'll have te fork that pile and haul some over where he laid and all. Gonna be a long night and a longer day fer me. Still, it ain't gonna be fun fer you to trundle that there heavy barrel downhill none either."

"Agreed," Jez said. There was no time to inform Antonia or Jez's mother of what was going on, and likely both of them were in bed now anyway. Jez and Jobah went off together in the dark to carry the body of the dead man back to the stable, where they laid an old tarpaulin held down by planks and stones over him in a back stall used for storing supplies. Then it was down to the warehouse with just the handcart to get the dried fish barrel, which Jobah admitted was a bit heavy for him to lift alone. It was a big one, but they would still have to curl the man up somehow to get him packed down inside and layer it with salted fish, and he was already pretty stiff.

"Ain't a big fella and on the younger side, but it's gonna be a tight fit and not easy ta git him down toward the bottom," Jobah said once they had the barrel on the handcart. "Gonna have ta take all the damn fish out furst too." He removed his palm frond woven hat and scratched his head. "I sure ain't lookin' forward to this!"

"Me neither, Jobah," Jez said with feeling, "and I am truly sorry to keep you up all night like this. You worked hard enough all day as it is."

"T'ain't nothin' I ain't had ta do b'fore, and that under the promise of a lashin' had I complained. Miz Antonia is a good woman, and yer mama helps her out a lot. They worth it ta me." He turned to face Jez. "B'sides, if'n they go, we go too, and likely back on the block to be sent to some plantation. I'd rather miss some sleep than face that agin."

It was a sobering thought. "We'd best get going then," Jez suggested.

Jobah grabbed some rope and then locked up and she helped him push the handcart back up the hill. It was pretty hefty, for the barrel was large and over half full and the way Jobah insisted they go to avoid guards was steep and rutted. They did not speak and kept their movements furtive but it took such a long time to get back to Antonia's place that much of the night was gone.

Jobah had blown out the lantern for safety in the stable when they left, but they would need light to see what they were doing. He yawned and stretched. "We gotta get us somethin' to light that lantern Miz Jez or we ain't gonna git this done afore dawn."

"What did you do with the candle stub?" she asked him and he pulled it from an old tin on the edge of one beam.

"I keeps a few in here jist in case we gets a storm. I got nothin' to light them with though. I kin go back and get a coal from our li'l oven, but I'm afeared that should I wake them gals they gonna wanna know what we be up to."

Jez did not think to bring a flint and striker with her either. "I can sneak inside the kitchen of the main house and see if the big oven got banked. My mother is most likely the only one to awaken; I'll deal with her if I have to. Can you find something to start putting those fish in while I'm gone?"

"Oh yeah," Jobah said, "I gots me some water buckets can hold a lot of 'em. I'll git right on that," he assured her as Jez went off with the candle stub in a holder and slipped inside the servant's entrance which would lead to the kitchen. She could see the big cook oven ahead and had to find a towel or rag so that she could open the door to the firebox, the handle of which was still too warm for even her own callused hands. It made a squeaking sound when she did and while Jez was poking around with tongs for a live coal, someone came up quietly on slippered feet.

"*Maman c'est seulement moi donc s'il te plait ne parle pas fort!*" Jez whispered in warning as she straightened up.

"No Jez, is me only," Antonia said in a low voice. She was wearing a long, thin night shift with an open silk robe over it. "The rest are asleep. Did you get rid of the... thing in the yard?"

Jez turned to her with the little candle stick lit. "Almost. Jobah and I are working on it. We have a plan and it will be gone by morning. It's best you not know any more than that. Now I have to get back to work," she added as she seated the candle it its holder before heading for the servant's entrance once more. "Try and get some sleep."

"You are such a good friend, Jezebel Johnston," Antonia said with feeling as she watched her go out the door and cross the yard to the stable. Then Antonia shut the servants' entrance door and headed up to bed, feeling just a bit easier in her mind that things beyond her ability to deal with were being handled by this very capable woman.

It took most of the night to find a way to get the body of the dead youth into that barrel. They had to undress him down to his small clothes by cutting away the fabric and removing his shoes to make extra room to get him packed well down inside. It was Jobah's idea to truss him tightly with rope like a fowl for the kitchen spit. The fact that the young man was rather slender and had partially curled up helped somewhat, though it was still an uneasy fit.

"Good thing it been a warm day or he'd have stiffed up too much," Jobah said as they were shoving in horse bedding along with scraps of clothing and the shoes to keep the body from shifting and making noise. "He gonna start stinkin' pretty bad by the time you get out to sea though," he added.

"So does the bilge. We might just drill this barrel and then weight it to sink out there," Jez answered in a low but unemotional tone. "It's better than he deserved."

"I cain't argue none with that," Jobah said. "By the way, I set aside the worst of the fish as was down the bottom, and all the extra salt. The salt'll help wit keeping the body dry and ye'll have something stinky atop if'n someone opens it up. How you gonna explain feedin' that to yer crew though?"

Jez chuckled. "You've never been aboard ship when provisions are running low. Hungry men will eat anything! I can always say we got it free, and we can use it as fish bait. It's what we'll have to do with it anyway, nobody is going to eat fish that have been atop a dead body."

"So, them men o' yours will know 'bout this?" Jobah said with alarm in his voice.

"Just that it's a dead man," she reassured him as they began to pack the top third with the salted fish, some of which were getting slimy. She looked at Jobah and gave a quick sardonic grin. "No worries, my lads are good ones, and they won't talk. After all, they're pirates now too, so they can't afford to draw attention to themselves or our ship. Like I said, pirates and sailors bury their dead at sea, so that should cover any inquiries."

"I sure do hope so Miz Jez, 'cause this is powerful unnerving to me. I cain't help thinkin' someone is gonna miss this here fella and talk will start over that."

Jobah had a point, but Jez countered, "Someone sent him to raid Antonia's house, and he was armed and willing to shoot. I wouldn't think they'll be bragging about that. Plus, he didn't look like someone who has fine relations who might worry about him. Let's just finish packing him so I can get him off the property before they do send someone here to ask about the incident."

With the lid pounded back in place, it took both of them grunting and straining to get the barrel up onto the hand cart. "How do I get this cart back up to you?" she said and Jobah gave a sigh.

"I'll send one of them boys down to pick it up in a while. You jist tell whoever is down there that it belongs to Miz Antonia up the merchant lane and they'll make sure it gits set aside. Me, I'm gonna have te haul that manure beddin' out by the barrow load, but ain't no big thing. I might drop some here and there, jist 'cause it tips easy-like."

He winked and Jez clapped him on the shoulder. "Jobah, you're a wise man. I'm glad Antonia has you to help her." She passed him a palm full of pieces of eight from her own purse, all of them cut small enough they wouldn't raise suspicion. "You hide that somewhere safe and use it as you need to."

"I'm mighty appreciative Miz Jez, and not so proud I can afford to say no. But I will drop one in the poor box at our church, 'cause so many colored like us got nothin' but sorrows and bad backs."

He helped her get the handcart out of the stable and onto the road as dawn was flushing the eastern sky. Jez began trundling it down the lane toward the main road, dreading how hard it would be going downhill. It was a well-made cart, cobbled together from wood the elder man had scrounged here and there, with high sides, two big wagon wheels on an axle under the middle which gave it good balance with a load on, and a squared U-shaped leg brace so you could set it down on a relatively flat surface. The tongue was short but thick with two rounded peg handles that stuck out so that you had something to hang onto and steer with. Jez was a strong young woman, but the load was heavy and the way down was steep. Thankfully it was not a busy part of the morning, because if she had to keep stopping for other traffic, it would have taken a toll on her muscles as well as her nerves.

She was sweating already even though the early morning was cool. It had been a long day and a longer night, and she'd had no sleep for over a day. Whenever she found a flat spot, she took a breather to get the pressure off her arm and back muscles, which were the only brakes the cart had.

She spoke to no one, just kept moving along. Other than a few early risers going about their business, there weren't many people around anyway, and none of those who had crossed paths with her had bothered to do more than nod and hustle onward. That was a relief, yet knowing she was actually trundling a recently killed man that some of them might know right through the center of the town didn't make it any easier on her mind. She figured most folks would see her struggling and figure she was too busy to stop and say hello.

By the time she reached the boardwalk, it got easier to move and Jez was glad. She was very weary by then and rolled her load slowly down toward the far end of the docks, where the smaller ships and bumboats were tied.

Now she began to run into busier crowds. The fishermen were already leaving, while sailors and pirates who had been out on the town overnight were staggering back aboard their ships or toward the boats that would row them out where their ship was moored. Jez was hoping she could buy passage to *Revelation* from one of them. Unfortunately, none of them were going her way nor did they have room for the barrel.

She was fortunate when one of her own men came lurching past. She didn't know his actual name, but everyone aboard called him *Soupy* because as ship's cook, that was the best thing he knew how to make.

"Hey Soup!" she called out to him, and while he was still fairly well inebriated, he turned around to see who beckoned. Jez waved at him, and he began to stumble back her way.

"Ahoy Cap'n, beg pardon but I didna see ya. Ye be needin' a hand there I take it?"

"I could use one, yes. Are you headed back to *Revelation* right now?" she queried.

"Aye, that I be," he said as he came over and helped turn the cumbersome cartload onto one of the docks. "Beppe said the bumboats should be out by midday with our provisions and he wants me aboard te say what goes where. Be this part o' it?" he asked pointing at the cask.

Now that was tough to answer. "It's something I got free that is spoiled, so it only might be good for fishbait. How are you getting back?"

"Easy enough," he said with a gap-toothed grin. "That darkie ye brought aboard was a good fella and 'e rowed me out. He took Beppe back last night and he's s'posed be on the way here with the crewboat te pick me up. I reckon we kin git that there barrel in the middle and sit close, though one more o' us mought have te row too."

"That should work," Jez said and shaded her eyes from the glare of the steadily rising sun. She could just make out the deck of *Revelation*, and there was activity aboard, but she couldn't tell if the little crewboat was on the way or not. She turned back to Soupy.

"Let's get this handcart down the dock and unload it. It belongs to my friend with the shop," Jez said, "and I promised I'd leave it with the harbormaster."

"Lemme take it down there fer ya Cap'n," Soupy said after a big belch. "Beggin' pardon mum, but ye look about done in."

She wasn't going to argue. "Just don't dump it in the bay Soup, we need to get it aboard," she said.

"I'll be as keerful as t'was me ole mum within, Gawd rest her soul," he said, and Jez almost burst out in hysterical laughter. He had no idea how close he had come to what was really packed inside. She followed him and gave him a hand getting the barrel down from the handcart. They placed it securely before the end of the dock and Soupy said he'd wait with it while Jez found someone who would take responsibility for Antonia's handcart.

She had to trundle the now-empty cart back a ways to find the harbormaster's little rebuilt shack and then answer a few questions before he put a note on the handcart and set it aside. Jez was heading back down to the end dock when she spied Soupy talking to a man in a guard's uniform. She began to hustle and then run their way as it appeared the guard was questioning what was inside the barrel and Soupy's voice was raised in protest.

"Well like I tole ye, I don't rightly know! Cap'n said twas goin' aboard and we jist be waitin' fer our gig te take the confounded thing back to our ship. Why're pesterin' me 'bout it? Cap'n Johnston's who ya need ter ask."

"And I am right here," a breathless Jez said as she loped down the dock. "What seems to be the problem?" she asked in as imperious a tone as she could manage, though her legs were shaking. This was what Jez had feared, someone questioning what was inside the barrel.

The guard turned to face her, initially not realizing he was speaking to a woman, for Jez was dressed as any pirate would be, with a hanger at her side and a pistol in her sash. "Well beg pardon Captain, but we've had a rash of things stolen lately from the swells up in the better part of town. So, when I see something out of the ordinary like this, I have to check it out. No offense meant by that, just trying to do my job."

"I am the one who brought this down, do I look like a thief to you?" Jez countered in an offended tone. She hoped he didn't notice her legs trembling.

"Look Captain... Johnston you said?" At her nod he continued in a more respectful tone, "I don't make the rules, but I need my job," the guard said. "I got a family to feed. Just let me have a quick look, and I'll settle for that. There's no bung to pull so I'll have to lever the top instead." He had a small pry bar tucked into his belt that was for opening crates and barrels and probably doubled as a truncheon as necessary. Jez had no choice because they were drawing too much attention now.

"Just please be careful not to break the seal on this, it's pretty slimy inside and I don't want it leaking all over my ship," Jez told him, worried that the way the barrel had tilted going downhill and from her and Soupy dragging it off the cart, more than just salt fish would be showing.

"I just need to take a quick peek within, and I'll be sure to reseal it properly," the harbor guard promised as he began to ease the head of the big cask open. "Phew, this reeks! What in blazes have you got in here?"

"Salt fish—some of which went bad, so they gave it to me to get rid of. We can always use it as fish bait."

"That's about all that mess will be good for," the guard said as he squinted inside, his nose wrinkled in disgust. He shook his head as he looked up. "It went bad because they didn't cure it right, you can see blood's been seeping up from below. Better you folks than me handling this slop," he added, tamping the lid back firmly down again. "I wouldn't keep it too long, it sure is smelly."

"That it is," Jez agreed wholeheartedly, "but the fish don't seem to mind. We might even snag a turtle or two on that stuff. Helps cut down on the salted pork or boucan I have to buy and it keeps the men busy when things are slow. I'm not fond of keeping too many live animals aboard, they take up room and make a mess, though everybody likes some fresh food now and then. Besides, it was free."

"Well Captain Johnston, you've a stronger stomach than mine," the guard said in an amiable tone as he finished resealing the big barrel. "If it was up to me, I'd heave this mess overboard and be done with it. Just not in the harbor please, we don't need more filth. You're free to leave and just in time too because it looks like your boat is almost here," he said and turned to walk off.

"*Thank God!*" Jez said under her breath and then let out a big sigh of relief. That had been too close! She knew what the blood in the barrel was from and it was a good thing the guard was put off by the smell or he might have been more suspicious. "Soup, wave Jengo over this way and have him snug up tight. We don't want that boat to move or rock when we're trying to load it." Getting the big barrel down into the crewboat was going to be tough, but Jengo was strong and rested, so the three of them managed after a bit of a tussle with it.

"I tied it down good," Jengo said as first Soupy and then Jez climbed down. "One o' you gotta row though, more for keeping us straight. Wind is up and there be some chop as you get out there. We don't wanna go over with this thing or we lose the boat."

"Oh no, no not that, 'cause I cain't swim," Soupy said with alarm. "I kin wait up the dock iffen you want."

"We'll be fine," Jez said as Jengo untied the last painter and tossed it aboard.

"I wouldn't keep it too long, it sure is smelly."

"I'll row with Jengo, you just sit tight Soup. We'll get there dry as old bones, I promise."

"Well these old bones I kinda favor, so I sure hope so, Cap'n," he said as he settled himself with his back against the barrel. "But I has te ask, why would we want a whole bunch o' slimy old rotten fish for bait aboard anyway? We don' do that much fishin' really 'cause we're always on the move."

"We will discuss it later," Jez said in that voice that told him that enough had been said about the barrel of smelly fish. She was tired, hungry, and needed a drink or three. The last twenty-four hours or so had been intense with one trial after another. Jez was beginning to look forward to leaving Tortuga, which just did not feel like home to her anymore.

She was very glad when they reached *Revelation* and Jengo said he would oversee getting the barrel aboard. "I want it stowed away from the food stores, but not so far back that we can't get at it," she told him. "I'll explain why later. Right now, I am about done in so I need some rest. Have someone wake me when the bumboats get here." She staggered down the ladder to her cabin and shut the door. After setting aside the fancy pistol and her hanger, she opened the gallery windows wide to the breeze and shed all her clothing but the man's blousy shirt she had worn into town and then pulled on some worn slops. Then Jez fell into her bunk and was almost instantly asleep.

It seemed like she had only been asleep for a few minutes, but Jez came instantly awake when Beppe knocked on her door and called out, "Capitana, the supply boats have come, they tell me you want to be up for that."

Jez groaned but slowly got to her feet and then decided she would go out as she was. "I'll be right up Beppe," she called while smoothing down her braided hair and tucking her billowing shirt into her slops. She pattered barefoot up the ladder to the weather deck and then smiled when Andy handed her a mug of cool bumbo. "It's a hot day Mum," he said, and she nodded her thanks. Oh how she needed that drink!

Jez had told Beppe to have the vendors line up on the larboard side, where the davit crane was being set up. She had also spoken to him about what they usually ordered from the boats, for he was not familiar with the foodstuffs which would be available in the Caribbean ports. The regular supply bumboats always brought a variety of items depending on the season. Plus, other boats hoping to make sales would follow them out, offering their own wares. Some even had live chickens and suckling pigs aboard in crates.

All monetary transactions would be handled at Antonia's end because they were sailing on her behalf, but Jez was asked to 'make her mark' on order slips that stated exactly what had been purchased. Unlike a lot of other pirates—including many captains—she could actually read, write, and do sums, so no one was going to get away with padding that account. She was also good at haggling as was Beppe, so between the two of them they got fair prices and only what they needed, though Jez did pay out of her own purse for some suckling pigs, extra fruit, and an additional hogshead of rum for making more bumbo. Tonight they would celebrate, for she hoped to sail on the afternoon tide the next day.

The sooner they dumped that barrel with the body hidden within out at sea, the better! All through the long day the thought of it nagged at her. That guard who had come down to the dock to check the contents had just about unnerved her, and what he said about people stealing from the wealthy hadn't made it any easier. Jez kept wondering if someone had already spoken to Antonia about the attempted robbery. Hopefully the nervous woman told them the right things! What if Jobah had not managed to cover up the blood in the backyard? Or her mother or one of the children had spoken up and said something they shouldn't have?

With all that on her mind, Jez had almost forgotten about her dealings with Sol at the brothel where young Carline was living until Jengo came up to her during a lull.

"I hate to ask, but what did you do to Sol?" he quipped with a toothy grin that showed some gold.

"I just faced him down. Why—did he come out to the ship?" Jengo shook his head.

"No, I see him at the docks when I pick up your quartermaster last evening. Sol tell me he gonna complain about you and your crew signing his own men aboard. He mean me you know. He di'n't have no one else but me after Mouse leave."

Jez gave a sardonic laugh, for that was the least of her worries at the moment. "Sol is all full of himself. If a man decides he wants off one ship and signs with another captain while in port, that's up to him. Your trip was over, so who you sail with next is your business. I thought you were talking about the run-in I had with him last night."

"Why? What happen?" Jengo asked as he helped steady a load of barrels in netting that were coming aboard via the davit crane so they could be set down without damage. He and Jez worked together getting the net unfastened so the men could take them down to the hold. She called out to a crewman first.

"Willy boy, that last one stays up top, find a shady spot for it or throw old canvas over it. That's for our bumbo tonight." That got her a few cheers from various men nearby and she chuckled. Then Jez turned back to Jengo, who was tossing the bunched netting attached to the line over the side for the next load and spoke quietly.

"What he said to you must have been before I ran into Sol. When I came in town, I went directly to that brothel you mentioned, intending to buy Carline's freedom." That gained her another big smile. "That old witch of a madam refused to talk terms so we argued some and then Sol showed up. He knew who I was right off and let me know that this Corbeau fellow owns the place now and that Sol himself has been put in charge. We exchanged a few choice words and we both pulled blades, so I got escorted out–"

"So, you couldn't free her," Jengo interrupted with a scowl, but Jez put a gentle hand on his shoulder and gave it a squeeze.

"Let me finish." She told him about her talk with Horace at *Aphrodite's Pearl*. "Horace understood the situation and will deal directly with Corbeau. I'm sure he'll be able to buy her freedom."

"I hope so. Carline don't deserve the kinda life she got there," Jengo said with anger in his voice. "She just barely past a chile."

"Jengo I know, but we have to be patient. Horace will work something out and, at his place she will be treated well. He's a good man," Jez reassured him. "Now let's get the rest of this stuff aboard and loaded."

She purposely said nothing to Jengo about Sol bragging that Carline was now his own personal whore to do with as he pleased. That would have only stoked the big man's anger, and he'd likely slip off and call Sol out over it. They didn't need any additional reason for the authorities in Tortuga to come out to her ship.

Once everything was all up on deck and the bumboats had left, it took most of the afternoon to get those stores in place. Meanwhile Jez sent a few men who could be spared out with the pirogue to get them fresh water in tight barrels. When they came back, a couple of the barrels were carried aboard the slender dugout while the rest were roped and towed behind, for fresh water is lighter than salty sea water and even in barrels will float easily enough. Those also had to be hauled aboard and then the crane was moved back to the rear to lift the pirogue aboard once more.

A sobered up Soupy had spent his time on the starboard waist, butchering and prepping some of the piglets for a feast. The butchering was done on the weather deck where the blood could be sluiced into the scuppers and the unwanted solids tossed over the gunnel. Then pans and buckets with the cleaned piglets and any edible offal were hauled down to the galley, which was amidships, just out of the way of the officer cabins. Two of the trusted younger lads had been busy carefully starting the fire with pine twigs and twists of dried dune grass and then stoking it with dry wood gathered ashore to burn down into the coals that were best for cooking. *Revelation* had a small iron galley stove on legs set atop a wide bricked off area filled with sand that was moistened before any cooking began. The pipe for smoke went up through the weather deck and it had been a favorite warming spot for the crew on cold Northern Atlantic days. The stove had large and small bake ovens, three inset burner openings for pots used for boiling or stewing, and a firebox that heated them all. The small but well-laid-out galley area had numerous enclosed shelves. Overhead hooks held utensils and pans with handles along with foods like fresh caught fish or strings of dried sausages. Barrels that held flour, dried beans and peas, salt pork, and ship biscuits lined the walls beneath the shelves where they could be quickly roped in place, a precaution against heavy seas. Braids of onions, garlic, and dried hot peppers hung from nails and two small lanterns on either end were kept in gimbals so that the cook and any helpers could see what they were doing. The prep table was bracketed against one wall and had drawers under the stout top surface that held cutting boards and a selection of knives and cleavers. That tabletop had often served as an emergency surgery site as well. Jealously guarded by Soupy was his supply of spices in a small chest hidden away because they were hard to get and expensive when purchased. In the past, only the officers aboard were given the most highly spiced food. The rest made do with plain fare.

It was different for pirates though, because unless the captain had someone aboard who needed to be impressed, everyone ate the same way. It had been an adjustment for the man who was used to cooking two classes of food. Yet Soupy loved his cooking and so tonight he would be preparing them all, "A right smart feast!"

Two levels of food and drink depending on rank was the way aboard most naval ships, and it was even worse aboard merchant vessels where the crew got the worst food imaginable and only a modicum amount at that. So it was with great pleasure that these men who had much experience as common sailors realized they ate and drank the same fare as their captain did, and unless there were shortages they could have all they wanted. Jez did not tolerate sloppy drunkenness aboard because that could cost lives, but compared to what these men had known previously, she was incredibly generous. They had done their share of boasting about her in port, which made other ship's crews either uneasy, unbelieving, or just plain jealous.

Jez didn't care what other pirates or the people ashore thought of her, as long as she was allowed into port to unload and get her cargo transferred up to Antonia's shop. At least then her friend and Jez's family would have a roof over their heads with food on the table while Jez and her crew would have enough coin to enjoy themselves in port afterward. That her gaggle of siblings would get some kind of education because Antonia had taken them in would hopefully help them not only avoid knowing the misery of slavery or settling for work that was all backbreaking drudgery, and for her tiny sister to avoid being stuck with life in a brothel. That made the risks Jez took, the wagging tongues, and the enemies she might make all worth it.

As a well-experienced pirate now, Jezebel Johnston realized that her privateer father had been a generous man who must have cared deeply for her mother. He had not only bought Monifa's freedom but supplied her with both coin and some education so that the former Negro slave could better herself. Monifa had worked hard all those years when Jez was growing up, making sure her eldest child by the man who had done her a great turn valued her own freedom and education as well. Jez would pass that inheritance of ambition and drive to have a better life onto her younger brothers and little sister, who were likely the only family she would ever have. This was also why she was eager to help Jengo free his young lover from that seedy bordello before things grew worse for her and like the others, she just learned to stay drunk and hoped not to wake up one day.

Jez put aside her deep thoughts that eve to celebrate with her lads. It was a lively night of feasting, with drinks for all and plenty of boasting. They made merry with tin whistle, drum, and fiddle music for singing and dancing. They were far enough off the shoreline of Tortuga not to be bothersome, even when it got loud and boisterous. While everyone aboard was tipsy, nobody became so drunk that they would be useless on the morrow. This was the way a good captain handled a ship and crew. That she danced carefree barefoot reels and jigs with even the least of them aboard further endeared her to her men. The crew of *Revelation* already knew that Captain Johnston always had their backs in battle, but now they understood that she was actually one of them as well.

CHAPTER FIVE

A watch had been set, and Jez and the others went to their bunks or hammocks. The call to rise came earlier than many of them would have preferred, but only a few were very badly hungover and most still in high spirits. It had been a short stay, but a good one—for the crew at least.

Once a bleary-eyed Jez was up and dressed, the enormity of this undertaking hit her. Not only did she have to get rid of that dead body in the barrel, but they had to find enough plunder to keep Antonia's shop filled. Planning a route was not going to be easy, for she still had a dull headache from all the bumbo and revelry of the night before.

She would have liked to see Antonia, her mother, and her siblings again, and to check in with Horace about the purchase of young Carline from the neighboring brothel. Then there was the problem of Sol and his mysterious benefactor, Monsieur Corbeau. Yet there was no time left to linger in port. Their ship needed to get back out to sea and pick up more lucrative prizes—especially since Walter and *Sea Witch* had not come back to Tortuga. That was troubling too, for many calamities can befall pirates who are continually drunk and unwary, although he also tended to drag himself through port. They may have just stopped elsewhere and cashed in their share of the take for a good time or perhaps decided to go off on their own. So be it; she had personal business to attend to and let that thought squelch down any concerns she had for the man who had been her first love.

The ship was already bustling once Jez was out strolling the decks. Any mess left behind had been cleaned up, things were being stowed properly, and lines were checked and coiled. She accepted a *cann*, which was a small open pewter mug with a bulbous base and a low foot, filled with something hot and foamy. She took a sip and then another. It was quite good.

"What is this, Percy?" she asked the kitchen boy who had brought it, and he gave her a gap-toothed smile.

"It be flip mum. Soupy says he made it special fer ye and ta other officers, like he used te fer our ole cap'n and his men. 'Tis good fer the raising the blood needfully, Soupy says, and I seen him make it. He mixed some beer, rum, eggs, a little spice, and a goodly amount o' sugar. Then he puts the stove poker in. He tole me te say to ye Mum, 'twill brace ye fer the day'."

"I believe it already has," Jez said, smacking her lips, for she had thoroughly enjoyed it. "You tell Master Soup I am much pleased and that I said he should have one himself." She knew Soupy likely already had his own share as she handed the empty cann back to the little lad, who nodded with a wide grin and headed back down to the galley. There were still new things to discover about the greater world outside of Tortuga, and that thought along with the flip had Jez feeling quite chipper. As much as she prized the fairness of the pirate life, now and then it was good to be reminded that as captain she could indulge in the occasional privilege. She strode up the ladder to the quarterdeck, past the binnacle and pilot house, and joined Beppe who had just finished and handed off his own cann of flip.

"Good morning Capitana," he said with an exaggerated bow. "I was about to suggest we bring up anchors and unfurl and clew down sails, unless you would like dat honor."

"I would, Master Beppe. Why don't you ring that bell and let our lads know we are making ready to move out." That had him all smiles.

"I will do dat," he said with a quick salute and then stepped aft and gave it a few mighty pulls. All chatter stopped aboard, and men turned to listen.

"Well lads," Jez called out loudly from the quarterdeck, "tide will be coming in shortly so it's time we head back out. So, let's get some able bodies down on the capstan to weigh anchor, and some nimble ones up overhead to start working the canvas and lines. We head out on the crest of the high tide this afternoon."

There was a general cheer. While able seamen scrambled to their expected positions, Jez had a quiet word with Beppe, Paddy, and Archie. The other two had come up the quarterdeck at the sound of the bell so she motioned them over close.

"I've something to discuss with you three once we're well underway. Before dark falls, join me in my cabin," she added. "I'll have some food brought up."

"We be dere, Capitana," Beppe promised as the trio went off to their duties. Jez knew these were men she could trust to get her ship out of port and into the upper Caribbean again, so she went down the ladder to her cabin to peruse charts and see if she could come up with a profitable course to follow.

Yet sitting at her desk with a map unrolled and pinned down at the corners with various items, all she could think of was the body of the dead youth her mother had shot stowed beneath rotten fish in a barrel down in the hold. It had to be dealt with soon. How would the men of *Revelation* react to *that* revelation? And how would she explain it?

Jengo stopped by the captain's cabin right before the other officers showed up. Since he already knew about the body in the barrel, as she rolled up the map and set it aside, Jez asked him to stay for the meeting.

"Once we're out to sea, I'm going to let the men know what was in that barrel," she told him as the big and brawny, ebony skinned pirate sprawled in a chair much too small for him.

"You think it wise?" he asked. "We could just weight it with ballast and sink it one night. No one need to know what be inside."

Jez sighed and sat back herself, arms behind her head with fingers interlaced. "Yes, we could do that, but this is a good group, and they trust me. So, I have to show that I trust them. Part of that is being honest about what we're carrying aboard. I won't tell them the entire story; just that someone I know shot an intruder and asked if we could get rid of the body so there were no inquiries. We are pirates after all."

"You the captain, but I warn you, men in port get drunk and talk too much. Me, I don' like this idea. If was my problem, I keep ever'thing quiet." He looked serious and Jez nodded.

"I'll think about it. I'm at least telling my officers what's going on." She could hear them coming down the ladder as they spoke.

Jengo sighed unhappily. He knew Jez was headstrong and would ultimately do as she saw fit.

Beppe, followed by Archie and Paddy, sauntered in. Jengo got to his feet, giving deference to men who had been aboard longer than he had been. Plus, in his eyes they were all white, and that gave them privileges dark skinned people didn't get. He squatted on his haunches near the head of Jez's bunk.

Jez smiled and said, "Sit down lads, grab a seat anywhere. Food should be up shortly and then we shut the door. We've plenty to go over tonight."

The first few days out of port were always good eating for all aboard. Any perishables had to be used up. Any livestock aboard still had plenty of feed to keep them going until men got too busy to tend them, got tired of dodging messes and mucking out manure, or they needed the hold room. Then the animals became the meal. This time they had some hens and a noisy, nasty-tempered rooster, a milk goat with a kid, and a couple of young pigs.

"All underway well?" she asked Beppe and he nodded.

"Aye Capitana. No sign of leetle ship doh. Mebbe something happen to dem on the way back."

"Maybe," Jez said in a neutral tone, but she didn't believe it. She had noted when they unladed at the dock that very little of the small goods and jewelry and none of the coin had been stowed aboard *Revelation*. So, Walter got the greater part of things that were easily turned into cash or credit without having to do any excessive bargaining. That had helped sour her attitude toward him. Would he willingly beggar Antonia and her own family to have a rousing good time for himself and his crew in some other port?

If so, it likely would have been Port Royal Jamaica. That is unless they got fired on or captured by the Spanish...

A boot hitting the door a few times in lieu of a knock interrupted her troubled thoughts. Jengo got up to open it. It was Percy again, he was one of the younger lads they used as a powder monkey, who also helped the cook. He had brought them a big tray of food to share, which he set down on her desk.

Soupy had certainly put some work into this *goodbye-to-port* dinner. There was a layout of yet another salmagundi including some stewed turtle meat along with roasted chicken, boiled eggs, and an assortment of fresh fruits and pickled vegetables. A batch of crispy cassava bread rounds worked as plates and something to soak up the juices. Percy was followed by another boy holding a chipped crystal footed bowl with a sweet concoction that Paddy and Archie recognized as a 'fool' made with pureed fruit folded into a custard. The second boy also had a finger bowl of warm water and a ratty bit of linen towel over his arm, a stack of small half gourds cured as bowls in the crook of his arm, and tucked into his shirt front was a cloth wrapped bundle of serving and eating utensils. Both had climbed up from the galley without spilling a drop.

Jez smiled at the two youngsters, neither of which was into his teens. "Lads, you may tell Master Soup he's outdone himself tonight, and because you were so careful carrying it all up here, that I suggested you've earned a small confection each. Please shut the door on the way out."

Beaming, they tugged their forelocks and stepped out, quietly shutting the door behind them. Then they raced down the ladder like children again, and everyone chuckled.

"Ye be spoilin' me powder boys Cap'n," Paddy said with a wagging forefinger in a mock defensive tone as she began scooping up salty, savory, and sweet salmagundi onto cassava bread rounds.

"No, I rewarded them for being careful," Jez said with a self-satisfied grin as she passed food to all of the men and they began eating as she served herself. "They'll more likely be just as careful carrying powder under fire when it comes to that, knowing they serve a generous captain. Don't forget, there will be times when Soupy needs help with patching up injured men. That's a lot for boys of that age to face."

"Aye, but they're back street brats, liken to how I was at such an age," Archie said. "They've seen all sorts o' goin's on. Plenty of fights and killin's and so on to gawk at when ya gots no home but a dry spot in a doorway and no work but pickin' rags, pickin' pockets, or cleaning chimneys." Archie obviously spoke from personal experience, and it got everyone thinking about how they came aboard.

"I see such things when I was growing up in Genoa. Always I want to be sailor," Beppe said around a bite of this and that. "But de seaport, she was not doing well." He shook his head. "De plague took most my family. So much crime and killing dere too. So, I go aboard any ships ready to sail out to beg for work. The English, they harsh masters and if you Italian, they tink you love Lo Spagnolos, so you get treated rough. Me I don't care what dey tink, I work a hard 'cause I just want to be at sea! Almost twenty year now. I go from common sailor to helmsman and quartermaster. I never go back, dis is my life."

Paddy laughed. "I ran away from me home to join the rebellion, toward the end o' it I was jist one step ahead o' the hangman. So 'twas out to sea or die in some gaol awaiting a trial and getting hanged anyway. We Irish live with the sea all 'round us, so 'twas no adjustment. I hate the damnable English Monarchy, but aboard one of their ships was the best place te hide out. Who would look too hard at a Mick on a bloody Crown warship—'specially iffen he can blow things up right handy, eh?"

"You all know where I come from, you call it Africay," Jengo said in a low tone. "Slave hunters pay coast tribe to go inland and raid our village. I was little then. White men force-march us many miles in chains and collars to the barracoons. Then aboard ship, we sit or lay down, too close, in chains. It stink in there, many sicken. My mother, those white men on ship would not leave her alone—even with a swelling belly. She die on the way over, so baby die with her. They just throw her overboard like swill. My father, he was big man like me, he fight them so they beat and starve him. He survive but with many scars and they broke his spirit. He got sold on the block first day we get to Barbados. Never saw him again. They sold me next day, and I work the cane fields for mebbe eight years till I big and strong. Then one day I get my chance. I kill the overseer with these two hands," he held them up, "and I run like storm wind down to the docks and stow aboard a ship headed North. Buccaneers took it near Tortuga, they want the sugar cane and that ship, so they boarded and killed all the crew. Because I help them, they make me a Brethren. Never looked back since." Jengo's normally grinning face bore a sneer of defiance.

Jez just sat and listened. She understood too well what the four of them were saying. Tortuga in her younger days had been full of its own scenes of violence and depravity. Growing up in a tavern next to a brothel, you didn't remain innocent very long!

"My home port was never a peaceful place, and that really hasn't changed all that much," she agreed. "My Da was an English privateer, I grew up on his stories, listening to him and the other jack tars talking about their adventures. I ran away to sea because of that and for the hopeless love of a man," she could feel Jengo's eyes on her, "but found I loved the life on the account more than I did him." Jez took a breath and a sip of rum; it was now or never.

"So, lads," she began, leaning back in her seat, "here we all are. None of us are saints, but so be it. There *is* something I feel the need to inform you of though," she added, now that their hunger was sated and additional rum was being handed around. "You see, I've brought aboard a bit of a problem I need some help with."

Jez ignored Jengo's warning indrawn breath and unhappy sigh, keeping her eyes on Beppe, Archie, and Paddy. They waited patiently, all three figuring it was the big Negro man she was talking about, who now that he had told his story, was likely being hunted as an escaped and murderous slave. Jez swallowed another good measure of rum, wiped the back of her hand over her lips, and then took a deep breath before she spoke again.

"You all saw me bring a barrel down to the docks, you helped load it aboard and stow it down in the hold. I told you that it has some spoiled salt fish inside, which it certainly does. But it also has a body that we need to get rid of once we're out at sea," she added without pausing.

Only Beppe looked surprised, which quickly turned into concern. Jengo shook his head with rolling eyes, but it was the other two men who had the strongest reaction. Archie and Paddy quickly glanced at one another, and then both busted out in raucous laughter.

"Did I say something... comical?" Jez asked in a stern tone while those two were still trying to recover their wind. Both Beppe and Jengo were staring at the other two men with curious expressions.

"No Mum," Archie finally said once he'd caught his breath, though he was still choking back the merriment because Paddy couldn't stop his chuckling snorts. "But ya see, we knows yah well enough now ta understand yer like no other woman we've ever met. Nothing terrifies or overawes ya for long. B'sides, we've loaded barrels of dried fish that size b'fore and they ain't that heavy. So, Paddy me bucko here, he says to me, 'Archie, this damn barrel be too heavy fer fish, i'n't it?' And I replies to him that it was, so maybe there's a body stuffed inside. So, we pried it open, but it just looked like slimy old rotten fish and it smelt so bad, we nailed it down real good and had done with it. Damn but I should have laid a wager on that, knowing our captain and all!"

As irritated as she was at their flippant attitude, Jez did have to chuckle. Did she really seem that callous and bloodthirsty to them?

"De problem here be, how we handle dis?" Beppe said with a concerned frown. "We no can just toss dis dead one overboard like garbage!"

Jez bristled at that. "He tried to rob people I care about and then threatened them with a sidepiece when he was caught. Fortunately, he got shot first. To me, getting dumped at sea is good enough for him."

"Oh no Capitana—no!" Beppe said with a shocked look, while crossing himself. "You gots to do de funeral rites or de ghost come back to trouble the living aboard. Is very unlucky and wrong to dishonor de dead on land or at sea—even de bad ones."

"Beppe, he's not someone we knew!" she insisted, sitting upright and leaning forward once more. "Why then should it matter?" Jez was already sorry she had said anything to them. Sailors tended to be superstitious.

"It matter to God Jez, who put him in you hands." He was adamant. "Who among us be better den de rest? This is mebbe test of you faith, for as you have said, we aboard must also rob and kill in dis calling. God sees all and He knows all, so we must at least show respect for the dead. Is de proper way."

This was too much like the attitude Beppe had when ship they now sailed was named *MASTIFF* and Jez was about to change the name to *REVELATION*. The last part of the New Testament of King James' English Bible was named *The Book of Revelation*. Jez had learned to read from that book, just as her mother Monifa had. She had a goose flesh feeling about what Beppe had just said, also recalling when they were stranded in the doldrums, how the St Elmo's Fire on the mastheads had appeared after she had knelt and prayed for her ship and crew's deliverance. That was right before the storm winds had come to set them free. Down at the docks, she'd been lucky the harbor guard had not seen the body when he opened that barrel, and she had thanked God for that. So, Jez decided this was something she could not afford to ignore, for she'd been incredibly blessed.

"All right then mates," she finally said with a capitulating note in her voice, "you've convinced me. If we must have a burial at sea for this thief and would-be murderer, I'll allow that it can happen once we are well away from Tortuga. Yet how do we go about explaining it to the crew? They know the barrel was brought aboard but nothing was said about it. Won't they be suspicious?"

"We just say he died ashore and want to be bury at sea," Beppe suggested. "Most of dat is true. When he be wrap up so stinking, nobody gonna bother 'bout looking at him."

"So, who gets that job?" Jengo said in a low and suspicious tone. Jez laughed ruefully.

"I'm the one that brought him aboard, so I'll handle it. It will have to be done down in the hold over the bilge, because it's going to be sloppy and smelly. I might need a hand with pulling him out, sluicing him down, and wrapping him though," she added in a sheepish voice.

"I help you with all that Jez," Jengo said in an equally chagrined tone. "Because you just help me. From the beginning, you never shirk the dirtiest or most dangerous work aboard."

She smiled ruefully at him. "I would appreciate it Jengo, because he's wedged in there pretty tight. Yet don't forget lads, we're all equals on this ship. So, I'll never assign such a disagreeable task to another without pitching in. It's not going to be pleasant, because besides the stink of those fish, he was gut shot, you know how those go..."

Jengo nodded and the other three men quailed at the thought. This would

"It matter to God Jez, who put him in you hands."

be repulsively messy!

They drank a couple more rounds and then the men went off to their duties. Jez took a tour of the decks, speaking to other sailors—all of them were pirates now she reminded herself. She made sure they'd had a decent meal and at least some bumbo, but there were no complaints. Most had a good time in port it seemed and were ready and willing to go out on the account again.

As the sun set in the west, a waxing quarter moon rose through the darkening sky, and she watched as the first bright star winked to life. Jez was hopeful this trip out would be even more prosperous than the last as she headed down to her cabin to get some sleep. Tomorrow or the next day, depending on their progress and any ships they might encounter, she'd have to deal with that body in the barrel.

They made good progress with fair weather and good winds in calm seas overnight, sailing west into the Windward Passage. It took them past the southeast tip of Cuba, tacking gradually north-northwest with the Bahamas and Andros Island to the east. They were heading up toward the Florida Straits again.

Jez had the vague idea of seeing if there was any raiding at sea to be done well off the coast of the Spanish Florida peninsula. She had gotten the idea from the Portuguese ship they had captured previously, that the current out at sea there along with the windy westerlies were regularly used by traders heading to and from the Caribbean. Talking to or just listening in on conversations by other pirates in port indicated that there was increased shipping traffic up and down the eastern coast of the northern continent these days, and trade between the northern colonies and their brethren in Caribbean settlements was beginning to pick up. Part of the reason was the current the Portuguese were riding went well out to sea and made travel far faster back toward Europe, according to the older pirates and certified as truthful by the eldest sailors aboard her own vessel. The Westerlies made it easier on incoming vessels, for they avoided the Horse Latitudes, where ships could be stuck in becalmed weather. It all made sense, and so she decided it was not just a ruse to send 'Madam Pirate Captain' off on some wild goose chase.

Jez was going to find a way to make that current work to her advantage in coming up rapidly on other ships. Unlike *Sea Witch*, a small ship really designed for cruising local islands, *Revelation* was designed for open water ocean sailing yet was still small enough to be maneuverable. She felt she knew enough about the Atlantic area outside of the Caribbean to sail somewhat away from land to cut off trade ships heading out or coming back—and they seldom sailed without a decently filled hold. Of course they could run into another warship out there as well, but they'd deal with that if or when they had to. That trip to the East Indies had made her far bolder than men like Walter Armitage were.

"What course we be setting Capitana?" Beppe asked as she approached him on the quarterdeck.

"Head for the straits again. I think we'll ride them north-northeast and see what we may find. I'd much rather jump a trader coming in with a loaded hold or someone heading up north with cargo of sugar or tobacco that trades well down here, than hunt only in these familiar waters like everyone else is doing."

"Could dere be warships along the way?" he asked in a concerned tone, and Jez shrugged. There was the question she'd been expecting!

"There might be but we've a good crew and a fast, small ship. Unless we make a critical mistake, we should be able to outrun them. You must have come across some pirates in the East Indies. Yet this ship didn't look like it had been badly damaged at any time."

That made Beppe smile proudly. "Aye Capitana, we did be chase by de Barbary pirati a couple times as we come down de coast of de dark continent. Dose *quei figli di puttana*," he swore in Italian with a curl of lip, "dey scatter fast when we can come round for a broadside so quick. Dey don't just steal you blind, dey take de good strong men to row dose ships, work dem until dey drop dead. Dey kill de rest just to spite us, and any ladies aboard get ransom or go to brothels. Barbary pirati do much raiding of de coastal settlements back home. Nobody safe or sacred; not women, or children, or even de monks and priests. Dey even kill de little bambinis too young to work as slave."

"I myself have never trafficked in people, just goods," Jez assured him. "If the men on board the ships we raid lay down their arms, we don't harm them. I may be a pirate, but I am not a bloody butcher," she added curtly and turned to stalk off.

"We know de difference," Beppe called in a reassuring tone, thinking he had insulted her. "You treat us like men of value. Nobody aboard dis ship speaks a bad word against our Capitana. Best one we all sail wid."

"You lads are all like family to me," Jez called back in a loud voice as she strode proudly down the deck, and there were many smiles as she passed by.

It was a leisurely two day sail up the Bahama Channel toward the straits. Late on the second afternoon they hove-to in a fairly open spot just on the northeastern side of Cay Sal Bank so that they could be rid of the body packed in the barrel. There was a bit of drift but Jez did not want an anchor dropped in case they needed to make a fast getaway, for they were still very close to Spanish Cuba. It was far faster to adjust sails and secure the helm than to raise all that heavy iron in a hurry and she did not want to 'cut and run' and lose an anchor. As long as they remained in deeper water, they would be fine, for even with the leeward drift and some forereach, they were still barely moving.

That morning Jez and Jengo managed to undo the barrel top. After scooping out most of the still intact salt fish to use for bait, they dumped the liquid, slime, and rotted fish out into the bilge. Beppe, Archie, and Paddy meanwhile were explaining to the crew about the burial at sea they were performing that day.

"This mess stinks something terrible," Jengo said, wrinkling his nose. "But the salt, at least it help preserve him 'til now." They were working under a gimbal lantern that swung back and forth overhead with the lapping waves so it was hard to see.

The body had bloated and was curled up, so it was too tightly wedged into the barrel to remove. They had to knock the barrel apart to free the corpse and then lay the remains out on battens spaced out to drain off. It was sopping wet with clothing and skin discolored and speckled with salt. Filthy hair full of slime, salt brine crust, and bits of rotten fish obscured the face. Jengo went scrounging for some old sailcloth the rats had gotten to, and he was busy cutting it up into some semblance of a burial shroud while Jez sluiced down the remains with buckets of seawater they had hauled down earlier.

Jengo eventually came stomping over with what cloth he had come up with to size it to the corpse and then almost dropped it in his shock. His sudden indrawn breath got her attention.

"What's wrong?" Jez asked him in a low voice. "He looks far better now than he did when we first got him out."

"You don' know who that is Jez?" he asked in an uneasy tone. When she shook her head, disturbed about his reaction, Jengo set the sailcloth and his sewing kit aside, and squatted down on the other side to be sure. He nodded slowly and even crossed himself before he looked over at her.

"I know you ain't seen him in some while, but this be Mouse. What happen Jez, why you shoot *him* of all people?"

"I wasn't the one who shot him," she answered in a sick tone. She kept her voice low, no telling who might be in earshot. "He came to my friend's house, the one who lost her man in the firebombing, and he was going through her belongings, trying to find something. We don't know what he was looking for." Jez had suspicion, but she wasn't about to mention it now. "Two of my young brothers were home, so one kept watch while the other ran down to the warehouse to tell my friend and my mother, who were working in their shop. Those two surprised him and when he pulled a pistol on my friend, Mama shot him. He died out back."

"Aw damn Jez, that's no good for anybody," Jengo said in a low but alarmed tone. "He is white and has a wealthy family. Negro folk hang for killing one of them."

"Blast it Jengo, I know that!" she said through gritted teeth. "That's why he's lying here waiting to be buried at sea," she stabbed a grubby forefinger downward, "and not back ashore. I just didn't know until now it was Mouse. Why would he break into Antonia's home?"

"Good question. He sailed with me and Sol, but when we get back to Tortuga, we all be broke and hungry. Mouse's mother take him back in. The father, he not so thrilled to see Mouse, who gotta big mouth, playing lord and master to make free all the time with the serving wenches. So, I think he maybe get himself thrown out. Mighta been stealing from your frein' cause he need money, or maybe someone pay him to look around. Too much going on in Tortuga right now. My concern be if Sol hears of this, he will tell someone. He keep in touch with Mouse 'cause Sol know Mouse gotta family that has money and Sol need to get his ship fix."

"Well, Sol doesn't know about this," Jez said with a modicum of relief in her tone. "We were careful how we handled it. Come on then, let us get him shrouded and weighted so we can get this over with and sail on."

As they wrapped the still moist and curled body and sewed it up tightly with several of the smaller ballast stones at the base to sink it, Jengo caught Jez up on his exploits with Sol and Mouse. Jez had never liked either of the other two, but it was interesting to hear how they all had fared over the intervening years. She still had that fond spot in her heart for Dandy Dan Abrams and his crew aboard *DEVIL'S HANDMAID*, most of whom had died when the Spanish Galleon bombarded them with what she now knew was Greek Fire[1]. She had learned so much about pirating in that first season on the account—things she never would never have dreamed of experiencing had she not so boldly run away to sea at the tender age of fourteen. Back then she masqueraded as a boy, and being a tall and slender girl, got away with it for the most part. Now she was openly a female pirate, and captain of her own ship. How much her life

---

1   Chronicled in *Jezebel Johnston: Queen of Anarchy;* ISBN-10: 1-946183-08-3 and contained in the omnibus collection of the first four volumes of the Jezebel Johnston saga —*Jezebel Johnston: Birth of a Buccaneer;* ISBN-13: 978-1-946183-49-1

had changed since then....

"You and me Jengo," she said as they finished sewing fast the shrouding canvas and between them hefted the body to carry it up to the weather deck, "we are going to sit down one of these slower days with some rum and have us a nice long parley. I've got so much to tell you about too. You won't believe some of it, but it's all truth."

"I believe ever't'ing you tell me Jez," he said between grunts as they were taking the ladder up from the hold. "You always did enjoy the pirate life. Most fellas, they be like me." He stopped talking to shift the load so they could turn toward the next ladder, with nimble Jez being at the head end, walking backwards. "Lots of men go out to sea running away from somet'in'. You run to the sea to find somet'in'. Even though you was a girl, and most of us di'n't know back then, you work just as hard as we did. You fight with great joy too. Now you become a woman who can stand up to any man and hold her own, for you learn so much at young age and you don' waste yer time. I talk to your officers, I talk to the men, they all proud o' you and have great respect too. Almost nobody complain on this ship. You done good all 'round."

It was a big speech for Jengo, especially considering they had just climbed two ladders, though his low voice was punctuated with deep breaths from hefting the lower end of the shrouded corpse. Jez appreciated hearing it though, and she beamed a smile down at him. It was the first praise she'd ever gotten from a former shipmate. She was still faintly grinning as they came out on the weather deck and other hands came running to help out.

"Let's get this done lads before the sun goes down so we can be on our way again," she told those nearby. "I'll be back on deck once I've cleaned up a bit," she said and vaulted down the ladder to her own cabin.

Their burial at sea ceremony was fairly simple. A well dressed Jez, looking every bit like a successful pirate captain, explained briefly that this dead soul was a former pirate acquaintance who got into some serious trouble ashore, so they were burying him at sea to spare his family any further embarrassment. Beppe volunteered to recite the 23rd Psalm over the shrouded body. Though he could not speak it in Latin and no one else understood Italian, he paraphrased it into broken English. Even with his thick accent and him stumbling over certain words and phrases, his deep and grave intonation sounded properly solemn. Men stood around the deck with bare heads and downcast countenances, many of them muttering along and a few like Paddy making the Sign of the Cross. Almost all had seen similar burials before, so they took it seriously. Then the body of the unnamed young man only known to his two former shipmates, was dropped overboard by Jengo with help from Jez. The ballast rocks at his feet quickly took him down into the depths.

That done, Jez gave the order to set sail so they could be on their way. She felt somewhat relieved that the situation was over with. Carrying that body aboard had worn on her—especially now that she knew it was Mouse.

What the hell was his birth name? She had to search her memory as she headed down to her cabin to change into old slops and a tar-stained linen shirt, for the weather was hot.

It came to her as she changed clothing: *Neville*. Neville Felton. His father was some plantation nob he liked to brag about. Yet they had always called him Mouse, mainly because he was small and sneaky. He'd at least grown out of his undersized body though he was still rather thin. He had certainly kept the sly and tricksome side of his behavior. Jez would never have recognized him had Jengo not told her who he was.

Perhaps Mouse's death might bring some problems down the road, considering how Sol was still involved with him, Jez was thinking as she felt the ship begin to move out and headed back up on deck. Yet for the nonce, it was resolved. Right now it was time to think about hunting prizes. They had only seen some small inter-island traders or fishing vessels around the lower Bahamas, but busier waters were ahead, and so keeping a sharp lookout was vital.

"What orders Capitana?" Beppe said as she came up to the forecastle where he had a man with a sounding line on the beakhead. Her Italian quartermaster was always a worrier, but it often kept them safe. There were plenty of shoals and reefs in the area, or shallows where even a ship their size could get into trouble.

"Steady as she goes Beppe. As long as we follow the rest of this channel," she pointed ahead where the richer color indicated deeper water, making an arc with a long forefinger "it will dump into the straits. It's all fairly deep water from here on, so remain centered, where the current flows. We just need to stay away from land masses." Jez looked up at the sky, where the sun was sinking to the west. "Weather looks good for the time being, so let's make the most of it."

"Aye, I be thinking you would say dat," Beppe answered in a more cheerful tone. "I be glad to sail free o' dis area. Too many reef and sandbar!"

"I won't argue that," Jez said with a nod. "We do have to remind our lads up top to keep a sharp eye out for sails. Maybe we could post one of the boys up in a crosstree to keep watch as well. Give them something important to do."

"Not a bad idea," Beppe said with enthusiasm. "I will have Paddy send them up and make a rotation shift of it. Keep dem all out of trouble, eh?" he added with a wink.

"That'll help I'm sure," Jez said with a laugh, and clapped her quartermaster on the shoulder. "I'm going to have Archie give them some target practice as well, and I'm thinking Jengo can show them how to use a cutlass and a boarding pike. He's quite good with a blade and deadly with anything else."

"He as good as you Capitana?" he asked as she turned to walk away, and she turned back and smiled.

"He's one of the best I ever trained under," she said, trying not to think about Walter Armitage, who as a former soldier was the best strategic fighter she'd met so far with both a blade and a rifle. Pushing Walter from her mind once more, Jez headed back down the deck to speak to her other two officers.

It was high time the youngest aboard were taught how to defend themselves along with their brethren and ship. They were a little too young for boarding and hand-to-hand melee fighting, but the sooner they learned to handle a weapon, the safer they'd be. Nobody on a pirate ship was given any quarter unless they could prove they had been captured against their will. These were poor boys, likely taken off the streets of some city and impressed into English Navy service, so no one would speak for them. If captured by the English, they'd hang just like the rest of her lads. If they had to defend themselves, they'd need at least some rudimentary fighting skills or they'd die quickly and that also would weigh heavily on her conscience. Unlike other pirates, Jez valued even the least amongst her crew as human beings.

She put that thought out of her mind for now too. *Revelation* could outrun a lot of warships, and she was shallow enough in draft to be able to dodge around into coastal waters where a warship couldn't follow. They didn't use these brig-rigged pinnaces for packet ships because they were slow—plus they were seaworthy enough to take long voyages. When you're carrying important correspondence and potential payrolls let alone transporting dignitaries, speed and maneuverability was all-important. Those were good attributes for pirating as well.

We're on our own now, and Antonia is depending on us, so we have to do well out here, Jez was thinking as she strode the deck, still dressed in working clothing like the rest of her crew. She put on a positive face, nodding and smiling at her lads as she passed by, looking for all the world like a tall and slender young man who was very sure of himself.

Things have really changed down here. We've seen nothing worth chasing so far and that concerns me. I'll not raid neighboring settlements like the others on Tortuga, and bring more trouble to my home port for this ship which is easily marked as mine. We'll go up the coast a ways I suppose, looking for traders coming in or going out, but we may have to go back out into the open ocean to cut them off. I just don't want to hit those doldrums again. Wish I had more charts! According to Walter, this is the storm season for the big blows that come across from Africay, which then angle northward. We'll have to watch out for those too. Yet we've got to secure another good haul or it'll all be for naught. Ah, for a bit of good fortune right now!

Nothing ever came easy in the pirating trade.

Little was forgiven amongst rival pirates either.

Sol was sitting in a low-priced tavern that was still operating inside a canvas tent, drinking their watery rum and growing progressively more bitter about his lot in life. He no longer referred to himself as Captain Peter Solomon, for his wreckage of a ship down in dry dock had made him the laughingstock of the remaining Tortuga buccaneers.

He blamed Jez for most of his problems. Sol was furious that she had called him out in public. The story of what had happened in the brothel had made the rounds of their brethren, most of whom seemed to find it amusing that he couldn't even intimidate a woman at swordplay. Plus, now she had convinced his only trustworthy crew member to sail off with her. Who knew what false promises she had made Jengo? Sol sorely needed the former slave's large size, fierce demeanor, and fighting skill aboard his own ship once it was seaworthy again, along with his affable port personality to bring in new men to sail with them. Yet even the hulking negro seemed to prefer the ship of the celebrated Captain Johnston.

How much time those repairs on his ship were taking was frustrating to Sol as well. There was so much rot on the old brig that they were damn near rebuilding it from scratch. Fortunately, he didn't have to pay for it—at least not in coin, though he would no longer own the ship once it was refitted and seaworthy. Sol owed many such favors to Corbeau now, the most important of which was to find that Bible that had belonged to the homely Spanish paramour of the Frenchman Lucien Lévesque had tortured for that information and eventually executed in frustration. What that Bible's importance was, Sol had been told, was Lévesque's business and none of theirs. If Lévesque wanted it, it must be found. It had to be turned over once *The Butcher of Bayonne* came back from his latest excursion out to raid along the Spanish Main or someone's head would roll.

Sol had sent Mouse after the Bible, for the sneaky little delinquent excelled at slipping in and out of his own home and he seemed quite skilled at pinching things when he needed coin. Sol himself had chosen the day and time, for he had confirmed that the women of the Spanish household were down at the warehouse and the servants were in the town for the weekly marketing. He had seen Mouse off but the unreliable little wretch had never reported back. Probably found a pretty bauble or two to buy the favors of another poxy serving wench and forgot all about what he was there to do. Still, Sol had to report to Corbeau soon, so he'd best have something to tell the man.

Word in the port had it that Jez was close friends with that Spanish woman. Sol really did not want to go back and threaten Antonia himself, she had friends amongst the plantation owners, and she'd likely call the watch on him. That would get him thrown into the fort gaol, if not out of port altogether. Sol could not afford to hire anyone else and Corbeau was not about to pay anybody on Sol's behalf. Still, there had to be some means to throw a scare into the Spanish woman—and maybe that arrogant mulatto bitch Jez as well.

Perhaps there was a way to get rid of Jezebel Johnston altogether! What if he told Corbeau she had taken that Bible out to sea? If Sol could somehow prove that Corbeau might arrange to give him a small, fast ship and crew to chase her down. If Jez perished in the battle, her ship would be forfeit, for all of her crew were English Navy men who had minimal experience dealing with pirates.

Sol made up his mind then what he was going to do. Even if it was fruitless in finding the Bible that Lévesque was seeking, if all went well, he'd have his own ship and crew and could encourage Jengo to rejoin him. Together they could sail off and go back out on the account once more.

A trip down to the docks first might prove worthwhile. There were men there who had seen Jez leave. He'd ask some pointed questions about what exactly she had loaded aboard.

After talking to the head of the harbor guards and getting a rough idea of what was loaded aboard that small ship of Captain Johnston's, Sol went to his cramped room over the brothel and cleaned himself up. He changed out of his ragged and tar-stained clothing, shaved, and after combing most of the lice out, tied back his greasy light brown locks. Satisfied he was attired well enough to be respectable, he went directly to Corbeau's elegant residence late that evening, knowing he would find the man at home. In Tortuga Monsieur Corbeau did not mingle too much, for he was somewhat of an outcast with the wealthy merchants and plantation owners. Nor was he popular amongst the buccaneers as he was a staunch defender of Lucien Lévesque. It was rumored that Corbeau was in trouble with Captain Morgan in Port Royal Jamaica, unwelcome in Charles Town on New Providence Island after a duel that killed a man, and had been recently exiled from La Grenade; so, he was labeled an instigator and provocateur best avoided. Corbeau currently dwelt in the middle part of the slope on that rocky, mountainous island north of Hispaniola. That area was where most businessmen had their homes.

The mysterious man lived in a rental house that was somewhat spare in size on a small lot, though well-appointed within, with formerly handsome furniture that was now showing some wear. Throughout the downstairs rooms there were some articles of art his landlord had collected in his travels. The owner was seldom home because he was a widower with no children who acted as a purchasing agent for those merchants who sold to the wealthy, so was often out at sea for months at a time. The property did have a well-kept garden and small yard as well as a summer kitchen, with a small thatch roof slave cabin attached to a shed large enough for a horse and two-wheel chaise out back. The absentee landlord had some previous acquaintanceship with Corbeau, so had invited him to stay as a caretaker of sorts. He had left behind several slaves, putting them at his 'nouveau concierge's' disposal.

Sol was made to wait in an outer room while the well-dressed, lighter-skinned male slave who had the house steward position strode off to tell the present master he had a caller. Corbeau did not hurry for anyone, but he did not drag his feet this time either. A lean man of middle height, he had obviously been practicing fencing for he wore a billowy linen shirt with some sweat stains, sashed in red and tucked into loose cotton knee breeches of brown over dark hose with buckle shoes. His wavy, medium-brown hair was center parted and trimmed just below the ears, though it currently hung damp and drooping with wispy tendrils stuck to his forehead. His beard and mustache had curled from overheated perspiration. He had tucked a rapier into its scabbard in that sash and now cocked an eyebrow over a crooked nose at Sol. "Let us go sit inside mon ami," he said in French-accented English and inclined his head toward the entryway to the living quarters.

"Send the boy to me with a fresh shirt. Bring us wine in ze library," Corbeau told the house steward as they exited the antechamber. He motioned Sol to come with him, and did not see the face the pirate made. Sol was not fond of wine, but this was Corbeau's home. He'd drink it and not complain, because at the moment he needed leniency from his erstwhile employer.

As they entered the library, a young dark-skinned valet came bearing a far cleaner and well-pressed shirt of linen. "Pardon-moi while I change. I needed the workout though I detest the feeling of stickiness afterward," Corbeau said as he untied the sash and handed that and the sheathed rapier to the little lad and then shucked off the sweaty shirt and tossed it at the child as well. "Rangez-les correctement. Allez-y maintenant!" he snapped, and the youngster nodded with fearful eyes before quickly retreating.

"I have no idea how my landlord puts up with these imbeciles," Corbeau said as he pulled the shirt over his head and tucked it into his breeches. "They are always slow to respond. They could all benefit from the touch of a whip now and then," he added as the house steward bearing the wine and two glasses came in. Corbeau pointed to a small, low table. "Set it down there, Jean-Pierre, then leave us and shut the door. I'll ring if I need something."

Sol had just nodded because he wasn't here to discuss house servants. With his minimalist dress and penchant for changing clothing in front of a guest, he had noted Corbeau was missing part of his left ear and had a not very old shoulder injury that had been crudely stitched. Unless all that had happened in battle or during a duel, those injuries along with the crooked nose said that this Monsieur Corbeau was no genteel businessman. For all his carefully constrained menace, Corbeau had some sort of sketchy background. That kind of thing could easily be exploited.

"So, what news have you for me, Solomon?" Corbeau asked as he handed over a stemmed glass filled with some deep red vintage that tasted acidic and was dry and bitter on the tongue. No wonder the French sipped it daintily like old matrons with their boiling-hot sugared tea! Corbeau was certainly living it up on Tortuga though, considering he was getting into his host's wine storage.

"Well, it's not as good as I hoped," Sol reluctantly began, setting down his glass carefully. "It seems my former trustworthy lad is nowhere to be found. Not sure where he got off to, but since we came ashore; he's had a constant hunger for willing young wenches and buys their favors with any baubles he can pinch for them. I doubt he'll bring us anything now. I'll thrash him well when next our paths cross."

"See that you do so," said Corbeau with a squint-eyed frown over his glass. "So, you are telling me you have nothing to relate about your latest assignment?" It was said in a lighter tone with a crooked smile that did not reach Corbeau's eyes.

"It's not entirely that bad," Sol answered warily, hoping to pique his interest. Corbeau leaned back and gave him a wary look that hovered between annoyance and curiosity. Sol gulped some more of the wine down then sat forward to explain. "Ye see, I used to sail with a colored lad named Jez—at least I thought he was a lad for a bit back then. Turned out to be a girl instead. She's now somehow got her own ship and crew and calls herself 'Captain Johnston'. She's a friend of Émilien's Spanish paramour, and she lured my other mate, that big darkie Jengo, to go back out on the account with her. Something tells me Jez might be the one with that Bible you said that Lévesque wants. Give me a fast ship and a ruthless crew and I'll go after them for you."

"And what proof do you have of zis potential chicanerie?" Corbeau asked in an acerbic tone as he sat forward to pour himself another drink.

"Just what she insisted on taking aboard for herself," Sol answered as he downed the rest of his own wine. Corbeau did not offer him anymore and Sol was glad of it because it was laying heavy in his gut. "I hear she had a barrel that she trundled all the way down to the docks by handcart, and they took it into her crewboat when they rowed out to the ship. Dock guard I spoke to said it was reported to be filled with stinking salt fish gone bad and slimy. It reeked so bad it gagged him. What in hell would they want with that unless it was a way to smuggle something aboard?"

Corbeau put his head back and laughed uproariously. "You are trying to convince me that this so-called female pirate capitaine is smuggling a valuable family Bible out of Tortuga in a barrel of rotted salt fish? Isn't that a bit... absurd?"

"For most people it would be," Sol retorted, "but the handcart was returned to Émilien's darkie servant. This Jez is a bold and tricksy bitch. If she spoke to Jengo, she knows that I made it plain to the Spanish wench that she needed to turn over that Bible. I'm thinking that she sealed it up inside and then took it out to sea; maybe for her own use, or to sell to the highest bidder. Her crew has been bragging about the many amazing things she did back in the East Indies."

That reference to the Orient made Corbeau sit up with interest. "You say zis woman is colored. Is she a rather tall and thin mulâtre with a prominent chin?" At Sol's affirmative nod, Corbeau got a speculative look in his eyes that ended with an ugly smile. "I believe I know zis one from an encounter not too long ago. She owes something to me as well. If I send you after her, you must bring her back alive with her fish barrel or at least its so important contents, and anything else that actually that might prove useful. For zis I will find you a ship, though it will not be not yours to command or to keep. You will be my émissaire aboard. Do not think to play l'assassin though, for my people report to me, and zey will know ze truth of it. You do not want to cross me in zis. Am I understood?"

"Absolutely," Sol answered, somewhat relieved.

"Zere is one more thing," Corbeau said in an introspective tone and a raised finger as he watched the man before him through slitted eyes. "Zis capitaine mulâtre, she has some family here on Tortuga, does she not?"

"Yeah, a mother and some by-blow brats." Sol was wondering where this was going because he was not up to murder.

"I have heard zey have moved in with Émilien's Espagnole whore, where she visits zem. Zis is true?" he inquired.

"As far as I know, yes. Why?" Sol asked with open curiosity. Corbeau gave him a predatory glance over a somewhat wolfish smile.

"Because you will take one of ze children prisoner aboard, and use it as bait. Make it a small one, though out of swaddling, so zere is little risk for it must be alive when she sees it. Zat will bring Capitaine Johnston to her knees, pleading for its life."

"I can do that—one of those little piccaninnies is always down the docks, poking around." They shook hands on it.

"You have much to do now," Corbeau said as he released Sol's hand, indicating their conversation was over. Sol was relieved and not at all reluctant to leave. To the experienced pirate, the look in the dark eyes of the Frenchman had gone from skeptical to feral, and now it had grown intense with a kind of lustful hatred that bordered on insanity. What could Jez have possibly done to engender that kind of eagerness in this mysterious man that was so often spoken of in low voices amongst even his enemies?

"Aye, I hear you." Sol replied. "When do we leave?"

"On ze morning tide," Corbeau said in a flippant tone as he crossed the floor to the door. "Go make yourself ready, find zat small one, and be down at ze docks at sunrise. Ze ship will be awaiting you. You will do your part aboard until that *chat sauvage* is captured. My men will bring in her vessel with a prize crew, but you will guard her and ze child, and whatever else she has until you deliver it all to me. If all goes well, I might then be encouraged to give you her ship and ze surviving crew she now commands; but she is all mine to deal with—do not forget yourself there."

Then he was gone, and Sol was led to the door and escorted out. He went quickly to his room at the bordello to repack his sea bag and hanger, still somewhat surprised that it was Jezebel Johnston who had somehow unwittingly gotten him out of a predicament this time by being her usual vexatious self.

CHAPTER SIX

I t took several days to sign on a decent crew for the ship that had formerly been Jacques Chagall's beloved *Danseuse*. In the meantime, it had been taken to a smaller dry dock to be cleaned, patched, and repainted, the figurehead and nameplate carefully removed and those along with the logbook presented to a convalescing and still weak and rather ill Chagall. It was then reloaded with ballast and guns, carefully refloated and towed out to the harbor to be held at anchor before being renamed and refitted as *Vixen*.

It would take another couple days to purchase and load aboard supplies. including rum and additional food stores. Walter Armitage and the ship's former quartermaster Arnaud worked together throughout, the two men comfortable enough with one-another now to present a united front as they interviewed potential crew members or negotiated for goods and services. In the evenings they roomed together upstairs in a small and somewhat rundown harborside tavern where there was decent food and drink at an affordable

"You have much to do now,.

price—at least for Port Royal.

The one thing that bothered Walter most was that he couldn't locate Pakke. The lad seemed to be nowhere in city. Inquiring after him, there was rumor the young man had been signed aboard one of Henry Morgan's flagships as a guide and interpreter, for the Panamanian Native knew the area in that thin isthmus pretty well. So that was another blow to Walter's plan of taking his ship back to hunting prizes on the Atlantic side of the Caribbean area, because ever-alert Pakke had always made the best lookout.

Now that the deal was done, Walter felt more than a bit uneasy about trading Antonia Campos' sloop *Sea Witch* and her share of the cargo for *Vixen*, for Henry seemed to expect him to join in his latest campaign. Those who traveled with Morgan would be paid in coin, but this would be a lengthy trip with a good part of it spent ashore, slogging through jungle growth. Walter wanted to at least bring in an initial shipment of salable goods to show off his bargain acquisition to Antonia, proving to her that he had her best interests at heart. He had grown tired of Morgan and his ceaseless bragging about his letter of marque from Jamaican Governor Modyford. Plus all the riches to be had by raiding from the Spanish mule and donkey trains that came through the Panamanian jungle at its narrowest point, hauling gold and silver from the western mines to the city of Puerto Bello. That, Henry had claimed, was how the Spaniards moved their wealth from the North Pacific side to ships that would eventually be coming into port from the Caribbean Sea. The plan was to get there well ahead of time and take armed troops of pirates through that area to waylay the unwary treasure train, with Morgan's men hauling the goods back to their own waiting ships and shoving off for Jamaica before any Spanish warships arrived. Henry needed plenty of men for that, for they would need enough crew ready and able aboard to handle the ships after sending large bodies of pirates afoot on shore—some of whom would come back injured or dead.

Henry Morgan consistently insisted that the new captain and crew of *Vixen* must join them, for the swift French corvette was well gunned and its ability to come about handily and slip into some tight spots made it good for reconnaissance. Plus, like Lucien Lévesque, he could now brag he had at least two ships and crew from Tortuga as well—the second being little *Sea Witch*, the small sloop they would be using for spying up rivers and along the coast. That was the ship, Walter found out, that Pakke was assigned to. When Morgan wanted something, he usually got it because he was not a man to be denied or trifled with. Many of the recently signed lads aboard *Vixen* had been eagerly discussing the riches to be had on crafty Henry's current expedition, so they also would become disgruntled if ordered to sail off to go raid in familiar territory where the prizes were now hit or miss and their share was split off from whatever was deemed salable for others.

Once the ship was back in the water, the final members of the crew hired, and everything had been stowed aboard, they had to make a decision.

"What do you think we should do?" Walter had asked Arnaud the evening before, when they were sitting alone together in the captain's cabin discussing it.

"That is a tough question you ask me, Mon Capitaine," Arnaud said, though he was pleased to be consulted on it. Chagall seldom did so, he gave orders that were expected to be followed. One did not offer Jacques any input unless it was solicited first or might be vitally important. The younger man sipped his rum and picked at some freshly baked bread, fruit, and cheese brought aboard for them to share before he answered. "I do agree with you about Morgan—for you already well know how I feel about him!" Walter nodded with a rueful smile. "Yet these men listen to his tall talking and they are seeing only the possibility of becoming insanely wealthy. They do not yet realize that Captain Morgan takes the largest cut for himself and gives much to his favored compagnons, leaving but crumbs for those below them. I would like to say let us go do our own pirating, but I think we must explain how we feel and yet put it up to a vote if we want a willing crew."

That idea gained Arnaud an unhappy sigh, as Walter sagged backward into his chair with his head propped on the top rail and fingers linked together on his chest. The lamp in the gimbal above was lighted yet turned low and so he squinted up at nothing. There was a long silence until he sat upright and forward again, draining his own rum.

"I hesitate to say it, because I'd prefer to just move out and go our own way, but you're right. We have to let the lads decide how they want things handled if we expect to keep them working hard aboard. We're understaffed as it is right now, though Morgan assures me he will send others aboard as he signs them up."

Arnaud frowned. "Oh yes, some to spy on us and make sure we don't plot against him," he answered in a disgusted tone.

Walter laughed ruefully. "I've no doubt you're right. Well, we'll put it to them as a vote tomorrow then," he added.

"It is the best we can do," Arnaud agreed as Walter poured them both another measure of rum and they clinked their mugs together before tossing it off.

The following afternoon, Walter called the men together over a barrel of bumbo and presented his options to them. He had a good idea what the outcome would be, but it was worth a shot to see if he could get a majority vote to move on to raiding without joining Morgan's group. Unfortunately, these men had never sailed with him, so they had no experience with his abilities as a captain. Arnaud was only known by a handful as Chagall's Quartermaster. They did know however the tale of how Walter got the ship, and the story of the altercation between him and Arnaud had spread well in the ensuing days. That these two had now settled their differences and were willing to work together was quite a turn of events. More than a few men were impressed that Jacques Chagall had been given back his figurehead, nameplate, and ship's log. Chagall was well known throughout the Caribbean for consistently bringing in fat prizes, but he had a reputation as a hard man who was could be a cruel and unforgiving captain, so most thought he got what he deserved from Morgan.

Henry Morgan was definitely the darling of the day. The crew overwhelmingly voted to follow him. Since Henry was now boasting he'd be leaving in less than a fortnight, there was no sense in trying to stall their erstwhile adventure. They'd prepare to be off shortly after Walter went back into town and signed on with the ever-ebullient Captain Morgan.

Frustrated but resigned, Walter took the skiff back to Port Royal by himself shortly after the vote, leaving Arnaud in charge. They had said little to each other before Walter left, other than what was necessary. Neither man wanted anything to do with this, but the crew did, and in the egalitarian atmosphere aboard a pirate vessel, the majority vote decided what they did next. At least that was the way Walter had always seen it done.

He tied up at one of the smaller docks and headed up past most of the more rambunctious areas of the harbor to where the better taverns were. That was where he knew Morgan would be found. All of lower Port Royal was abuzz with inebriated raucous men celebrating with shouts and gunshots while strumpets and pickpockets made the most of their time. There was singing and dancing in the rutted streets and open debauchery around every corner. The gutters and walkways were full of swill, piss, vomit, inebriated drunks, stray dogs, and losers in fights over women, along with a few who'd been robbed or had their throats cut. Everyone was happily celebrating Henry Morgan's latest quest-to-be.

Everyone except Walter Armitage. He was furious. What was Morgan thinking, bragging about this venture all over town? Didn't he understand there were spies and enemies about looking to report this potential raid to the Spanish for whatever gold or silver they could earn for themselves? Had he not the common sense to keep things quiet?

Walter found the celebrated Captain Morgan just by chance in Henry's favorite tavern amongst the most expensive ones. You couldn't mistake his booming, boasting voice telling some tale that resulted in roars of raucous laughter. Walter headed over to the *Silver Buckle Shoes*, its colorful sign bearing a nicely painted portrait of its namesake.

This was one of the few upper class establishments Morgan didn't own yet, though it seemed as if he was dominating the place, for as Walter came through the propped open door, the taproom was alive with pirates. Most of them appeared to be captains, quartermasters or other officers from ships in the harbor. They outnumbered the merchants, well-to-do planters, and nobles in the house by ten to one at least. None of these upper-class men looked very happy to have this too-well known king of pirates and his loudly braying seafaring cronies dominating the place, but Henry Morgan was not someone you had forcibly removed, unless you wanted your establishment to be signed over to his agent by morn. Once Morgan was crossed, it would be either sell out now or be burnt out in an 'unfortunate accident' in the not too distant future. Then he would buy up the lot and have someone build a new, even more lavish establishment.

It was fairly well lit inside, mostly by candle chandeliers well above the 0narrow dance floor. That space was banked by long tables with benches on both sides. There were some smaller round tables scattered in dimmer corners out back for small, intimate parties requiring quiet conversation. Lively music that was nearly drowned out by the noisy group surrounding Morgan came from a small stage area at the near end of the bar. A three-piece group with a piper, a fiddler, and a blind boy who beat a handheld skin drum with a wooden mallet had set up there with their tip basket out front. Walter stopped to drop in a few small coins and gained a nodded thanks from the piper. The bar was long and filled most of one side with the kitchen and storage behind it. Walter went well around it, threading his way through tables to avoid those thronging Morgan's animated group. The barkeep was a grizzled older man wearing a sour look, a dingy canvas apron, and an eyepatch, probably a former sailor or pirate. Walter noted he was missing two fingers on his left hand as he swabbed the bar and frowned down at the far end where the celebrated Captain Morgan was holding court. The serving wenches moving around the spacious room were all quite young and comely as well as provocatively dressed. They sashayed their way through the bustling crowds with trays loaded with pewter tankards or clay mugs of rum and ale, though a couple tables were having wine or other imported spirits. Some trays held food steaming from the kitchen hearth or cold plates of sliced meats, bread, and fruit. It had to be a pricey place to drink or sup in.

"Can I help ye, handsome sir!" said a smiling buxom girl with curly red hair and freckled creamy skin. She was considerably shorter than him and sounded Irish, her voice was lilting and a bit high pitched. In spite of his mood, Walter had to smile back at her.

"Aye you can, lass. Would you send my compliments and another drink over to Captain Morgan, and tell him I await him on his pleasure. I'll find myself a small table in the back and I'll take whatever Henry is having while I wait."

She gave him another winning smile and Walter felt his loins stirring. He noted that her teeth were good if a bit crooked and her eyes brilliant blue as she tilted her head to one side and her face caught the candlelight. "And just who shall I tell him be awaitin'?"

"Oh, right," Walter said with a laugh. "Captain Walter Armitage of *Vixen*. He knows me."

"Have a seat then Captain Armitage, and I'll find ye shortly with yer drink and any reply he sends, luv," she said before hustling off with swaying skirts bustled up over full hips to show some lower leg above her little boots. Oh, she was a looker, and it had been a while since Walter had been with a woman. Seeing Jez again and finding her haughtily cold and uninterested hadn't helped.

Dallying with women was best put out of mind for now, Walter had business to conclude with Morgan. Then maybe he'd have himself a rousing good time while still in port.

The redhead wasted no time in bringing his rum and a complimentary platter of odds and ends to pick at. "Captain Morgan says he'll be with ya shortly luv." She gave him a dimpled smile and a wink and then with a swish of skirts turned to hasten off again, but he caught her arm, and she looked back over her shoulder with a toss of her russet curls, though she didn't pull away. "Be there something else then Captain Armitage?"

Oh, could those blue eyes sparkle! She was certainly not shy. Walter shifted a bit uncomfortably in his chair, he was sorely tempted to invite her upstairs now for a tumble, but he had to see Morgan first. "You can call me Walter, lass. Now, what's your name and what time do you get off tonight?" he asked.

She smiled, the dimples deepening and then said in a low voice, "I be Fíona, Walter; but I don't get off until late because we're busy all the time here. 'Tis a vera long day."

"You leave that up to me. Watch for my signal on my way out. If I wink, you've got some time off coming."

"I'll do that Walter," her smile was winsome, and she blushed a bit. "Ye need anythin' else, ye let me know."

"I'm sure there will be something else," he said with a lusty smile and then she was off again, for the place was too busy for her to have time to dawdle and trade lascivious innuendos with him. Walter watched her go with a sigh and set in to having a few bites off the platter of food and drinking, taking his time to savor this high-quality rum he was likely paying too much for.

He hadn't even had time to down a third of his rum or make much progress on the food before portly Henry Morgan came threading his way through the throng to join him, a tankard in each hand. Morgan had on a long open-fronted ruby-colored coat thickly sashed at the waist with scarlet silk, worn over a ruffled sleeve, fine linen shirt with a frothy white lace jabot at the throat. He had donned his heavy baldric and belt with vermeil buckles; it held a fancy hilt cutlass at his left side, and no doubt there was a pistol and knife or two somewhere about him as well. Henry's tall black leather boots were well polished with the bucket cuffs turned up over tan knee breeches. His thick and dark curly hair shone with pomade oil that glistened in the flickering candlelight where it hung down on his shoulders. His earlobes and fingers were ornamented with good quality gold, the finger rings studded with large, colorful gemstones that winked as the light caught them. He was definitely in fine feather today, and he knew well how to make an impression.

Walter felt poor as a church mouse beside him, but then he wasn't here to impress anyone.

"Ho, Walter me lad, good to see you," Henry boomed as he approached. Morgan set down his drinks and yanked out a chair where his back would be against the wall and he could watch the room. That was something he was fond of doing since not everyone admired Captain Morgan as much as they claimed.

"Aye Henry, I finally had a moment to come in and sign us on to your forthcoming adventure," he answered, getting right to the point. He forced himself to smile back broadly so there would be no controversy in front of the other men, for he could feel their eyes upon him.

"No worries there my prudent friend," the big man said in a lower tone as he leaned back with the first of his two tankards in hand. "I knew you'd be busy getting rigged up and making sure your new lads understood their business before we put out. Plus, I figured with you being the cautious sort, you'd need to think it over for a bit." He gave Walter a smirk that lifted one bushy eyebrow and the corresponding half of his upward-curled mustache. "I'll be glad to have you and your vessel in my fleet for this is going to be one damn fine excursion for us." He took a sip of one tankard in his left hand and wiped his right hand over his thick lips, then raised that hand with fingers splayed out. "Imagine it now—riches beyond belief to be had with just a quick sail down to the southwest and a bit of a tramp into the jungle. They'll never expect us there!" He clamped his fingers into a fist and brought it back as if he already had grasped his share. "We'll do so well I tell you;

you'll live like a king for months afterward." He was certainly selling it hard enough.

Walter took another long pull on his own rum to help hide his cynical smirk; at least this was fine stuff, not the rotgut you got aboard. Morgan had already finished his first and lifted the second in a toasting gesture. "Now I appreciate the invitation to engage you socially lad, but you needn't have wasted your coin to impress me. I pegged you for a frugal man and I know you've had your doubts, but I also knew you'd come around to my way of thinking. So, we can sign the papers tonight if you wish and then you can celebrate on my behalf." He took a rolled scroll of some length from his shirt and then motioned for a young fop in a waistcoat and fine clothes with pince nez on his nose to come forward. His curling brown hair was cropped short, both mustache and pointed beard heavily pomaded and waxed. He had brought with him a carved and inlaid box. When opened, inside were compartments holding a capped inkwell, a fine knife for trimming the selection of quills, and some blotting material called pounce in a small but interesting carved wooden shaker. Henry smiled faintly at Walter's look of concern as the young man laid them out while Morgan himself unrolled the scroll to its latest signature. Henry did it slowly, showing off that there were a lot of other captains and ships involved, some who had signed with no more than crooked X's after the captain's name and ship had been written in.

"My scribe friend here, Master Exquemelin will witness for me that I did naught to coerce you nor did I alter anything after you added your signature and ship. As I recall you are an educated man who can do more than just make his mark." Exquemelin quietly laid before Walter the inkwell and handed him a well-trimmed and sharpened quill.

"Of course," Walter agreed between teeth gritted into a smile as he dipped the nib of the quill and signed away his next several months; if not his very life, ship, and all those aboard. He tried not to focus on what Antonia Campos or Jez would think of this or what potential clauses there might be later in his signing, for Morgan was sharing few details there. Yet it was the only way to keep this bigger and more seaworthy ship and have a willing crew. Exquemelin watched him write with little expression on his face and then with a nod from Morgan, he carefully blotted it with deft and careful shakes of pounce, only blowing it off onto a waste sheet to pour back into the container after he was certain it dried the ink. Then Henry took the scroll and scanned it with satisfaction before rolling it up again and tucking it away. Exquemelin packed up his material, bowed to Henry, and strode off.

"Ah now that is done, we need some more refreshment." Henry stuck his pinkie fingers into his mouth and whistled loud and shrill like the Welsh shepherds of his homeland would. When he got the attention he needed, he lifted his two empty tankards and waved them around indicating he wanted more rum.

The barkeep himself eventually stomped over and slammed down a couple more tankards, taking the three empties away without a word, though he looked daggers at Morgan and spit on the floor as he turned away. Henry only laughed, though his dark eyes went hard before he turned back to Walter with his tankard held out.

"Now my friend, we shall have our own toast to our alliance, and then you can ask me for anything else you need—within reason of course." They clanked their tankards together and each took a deep swill, Henry swallowing a good third of the contents without a breath. Good God, the man could drink! "Now then," he continued after wiping his mouth again, "what will that be? There has to be something you need or desire; there always is."

"That's very generous of you," Walter said in a wary but resigned tone. "All I'd really like is some additional rifles and pistols, more powder and shot for my boys—some of whom need practice badly, they are not soldiers after all. Oh, and um..." Walter glanced around the room. Morgan was patient though a little smile crawled around under his mustache, for he had an inkling what was next.

Walter spotted her. He inclined his head. "That red-haired serving wench Fíona? Think you can talk old One-Eye over at the bar into letting her off for the evening?"

Henry Morgan slapped Walter on the back before he threw himself backward in his chair and let out a loud and hearty guffaw of laughter. He rocked his chair so hard that he almost tipped over. Men who knew enough not to approach them turned to see what Captain Morgan was going on about now.

"Did I say something funny?" Walter asked with unease as Morgan sat up again, wiping his eyes and still chuckling.

"No lad, no, it's not that," Morgan croaked and gasped as he waved his hand dismissively. He took another long pull to wet his mouth and then cleared his throat. "You see, it happened that she begged me for the bloody same thing!" he replied once he'd caught his breath. "You must be some fine catch of the day for the lass, for all she is half your age, and you with no outward appearance of having much coin to spare. Yet here she is lusting after a man old enough to be her father with nary a sign of good fortune on his person. I already fixed it with her miserly employer, which is another reason he's pissing and cursing into my following wind. When you leave, she does too. Oh, I envy you, she's young and finely made, so have her once for me as well, eh?" Before he stood, he fished in his shirt, yanked out a purse and took a bit of silver from it. That got slapped down on the table and he tucked the rest away before rising. "Buy her a nice little bauble afterward so she'll be sure to long for you until you return. Now I have another appointment, so if you will excuse me, Walter my friend, I'll see you in a few days. Have fun!"

Then Henry Morgan strode off through the tobacco smoke and the fumes of liquor and roasting meat. The crowd parted for him as waves will to the bow of a gallant warship.

Walter watched him go and then with a sigh, took up his tankard and began to drink it down in random gulps. No sense in regrets now, for the deed was done. He was feeling the rum on his somewhat empty stomach, for Morgan had finished the platter of food while he was signing away his ship and crew. Walter would need to eat something else if he was to have the energy to tumble that bold Irish lass who was likely half his age, he'd already noted that she kept smiling his way.

Well, he didn't want to eat here, not on Morgan's coin. They'd go somewhere else together to find something appetizing but affordable. Walter needed to get her away from the oversight of her surly master anyway and then see how things went after that. Surely, she'd seen worse than the rooming house he and Arnaud had shared. His quartermaster would be staying aboard tonight so they'd have the room to themselves, and no one there asked questions.

He caught Fíona's eye and getting to his feet, stalked away. She looked to her boss and then catching his reluctant nod, she grabbed her cloak from behind the bar. Throwing it around her shoulders, she scurried out after Captain Walter Armitage, before he got too far ahead of her.

This one was going to be her ticket to a better life.

CHAPTER SEVEN

Revelation picked up the straits late in the day. Jez set a northeasterly course into the current that would eventually take them up around the end of the Florida peninsula, then if she had understood correctly gradually north, parallel with the continent. These were considered to be primarily Spanish waters, though ships from other colonies frequently passed through. Since she had heard there was now often trade—some of it definitely illicit— between the northern and southern colonies, she hoped to pick up some worthwhile prizes. Her ship might be on the small side, but since its hold had far more room than *Sea Witch,* what they brought back in could potentially be far more substantial. They had held quite a bit of furniture and household goods taken from that Portuguese caravel.

She was still angry though that Walter and his crew had taken all the prime small goods from that prize, for while she was kept busy translating, none of the coin, jewelry, or fancy ceramics had made it aboard Jez's ship. Well for good or for naught, it was gone now, and she suspected, so was he.

Because it was a fine day with generous winds and a following sea making for easy sailing, she cast aside her displeasure and misgivings to just soak up the sun and savor the breeze as she strode up to the forecastle, where she could lean out from the foremast shrouds and get a sense of where they were and what lay ahead. Compass in the binnacle and other navigation tools aside, Jez still preferred to look at the water, scan any land masses, note the sun's position in the sky, and at night the stars. That and some charts were enough for her.

At least the winds here were steady and could easily be adjusted for. Her main concern was hitting a becalmed region again, which is why she preferred to travel closer to the coastline where there might be a land breeze at night. There was always the danger of running into a warship, but that could happen anywhere. She had to chance it; they needed a decent cargo. Unlike Walter, she had strong ties with Antonia's shop, for the life and livelihood of the Spanish woman who became a friend and had taken in her mother and siblings after the family business was lost meant a lot to Jez. Their survival depended on filling that shop with things the gentry would be ready and willing to snap up at what to them would be bargain prices.

Someday, Jez mused, *I would greatly prefer to do trips out like this without all the battle and bloodshed.* Just how to go about that and still get good prices for resale was the problem. Piracy ensured free cargo but at a great cost of human suffering via injuries and deaths, along with potential damage to her ship. Plus, *Revelation* was rather small as cargo haulers go, though a larger ship required additional crew who all had to be paid, and being pirates they had no affiliation with any country's naval force for protection. Traveling to the East Indies took too long in her estimation, and even the manufacturing places in Europe and the Far Orient were all tied up by trade routes and tariffs. As far as Jez could tell, other than slaves, Africay had little to offer, and she'd have no part of trading in human misery. Other than rum or maybe sugar itself there was very little in the way of trade items worth bothering with amongst the colonial islands of the Caribbean Sea, for while there were some things being produced on plantations or taken from the land and water like gold, silver, or pearls, their distribution and potential sale was controlled by their mother country. It was frustrating!

There had to be a way to circumvent that without piracy involved. She would have to give it some serious thought. For now, living as a pirate was all she knew. Jez turned and stood with her back to the prow looking over her ship and her busy crew. She was fond of these lads and loved her little ship, she'd hate to lose *Revelation* in some encounter or have to watch her loyal men die in battle or rot in gaol until to the last man they were sentenced to die swinging, choking, and kicking on a gibbet until it was her turn.

Well, there was nothing she could do about it now. Jez just hoped her luck would hold. She headed back down the deck, nodding and smiling at men and boys going about their work, only stopping to show the youngest ones aboard how to properly tighten the lanyards on the triple deadeyes that held the shrouds in place.

"Put your whole body into it laddies, that's how you build the muscles you need aboard." She demonstrated by leaning back to help tighten a line, something Jez could easily do now without straining though they needed to see it demonstrated while she had the time and inclination to teach them. These three were still underage and mostly used to being cabin boys, cook's helpers, or powder monkeys—too young to be common sailors or midshipman, the latter an unneeded position aboard *Revelation*. On a pirate vessel, you learned it all, for you never knew when you'd be filling in for a man who was ill, injured, or dead. They each got a turn to try and all three agreed that it helped.

"Remember, on this ship, we're all equal, so we aid one another. You see a matey struggling, you offer a helping hand. You need assistance yourself or don't know how something is done, you ask someone. If anybody refuses to help you, you come see me, and I'll set that right. We all started out in the same place."

There was a chorus of, "Yes mum!" and some attempts at salutes, which Jez shook her head at, laughing and motioning that they put their hands down.

"You're not in the blasted Crown Navy any more laddies, this is a pirate ship and no need for that nonsense. Now off to your duties, I've some of my own to attend to," she told them, seeing Jengo and Archie heading her way. Since Archie was acting boatswain who had charge of everyday maintenance and training on deck, and Jengo was her arms instructor, she figured this was about setting up small arms practice.

"Wha' in blazes be these lit'le ingrates up to now?" Archie asked while giving the young threesome a withering glare.

"Nothing Archie," Jez reassured him, "I was just showing them how to use body weight to tighten the lanyards properly. They're a bit young to have the strength to pull it taut like a man would."

"Aye, these gutter whelps be naught but skin and bones," he agreed, crossing his arms on his chest and giving the three lads a good once over. "Ain't enough meat on 'em tuh feed the blasted sharks. Goes to show ya what flo'sam the English Navy drags aboard."

Jez had no idea what 'flotsam' was—maybe some sort of fish? So, she just nodded and replied, "Well aboard my ship we'll feed them and teach them all they should know. Right now, unless I'm needed up here, I'm going down to my cabin to look over what charts we have. We'll have to decide where to head next."

Jengo looked as if he had something to say, but before Jez could question him, one of the men in the tops called out, "Sail Ho!" He was up on the mizzen mast, so it had to be either a following ship or from where she stood considering the current sweep of the sails, one coming in from starboard.

"What direction it from?" Beppe yelled up to him from the quarterdeck as Jez hustled down the foredeck ladder with Archie and Jengo right behind her. She could tell by the accent who it was that had sighted the ship.

"Well off starboard, heading in behind us," was the reply from Liam, who everybody but Jez and Jengo called 'Skirts' because he insisted on wearing his raggedy kilt on board. "I cannae see who 'tis yet, just three masts; but 'tisn't a merchantman. Could be a warship, sartain to be big enough."

That would not do! "Beppe have the lads pile on some sail and raise the French colors. We'll outrun them, if possible," Jez shouted as she raced aft, pounding down the main deck, dodging men already dragging at halyards to get more canvas up and those pouring out of hatches from below. She continued to bark orders as she ran. "Paddy get crews together to man the gun ports. I want men on the stern chasers just in case we need to send a warning shot. Have anyone who can be spared down on the gun deck. Archie," she barked an order as she ran past him, "get those who are good with a long gun ready to go up into the tops. We want them to know we're serious about defending ourselves!"

"Aye mum!" he yelled after her and then hustled off calling for men by name to come with him. The three young boys were already headed down to the powder room, for they knew their duty.

Long-legged and nimble, Jez made it up the quarterdeck ladder in three bounds, where Beppe handed over the glass while pointing off the starboard stern quarter. "She be gain on us Capitana," he said in a worried tone. "Spanish for certain, galleon from de shape of her."

With her sharper eyes, Jez had taken a good look at it already. "Spanish coastal patrol," she said with some small relief, scanning with the glass. "Single gun deck with eight ports a side, plus fore and aft chasers no doubt. I only see only four ports open, all toward the foredeck. Should be the same on the other side to maintain balance. Not a lot of freeboard on this one, she's

"What direction it from?"

well loaded and low in the water. Can't tell if they have marines aboard but I don't see any armor. They've put up extra sail, so they're interested in us, but they're also acting very cautious in keeping their distance. Since they obviously are not full with guns, I would think..." her voice dropped off as she sighted what she could of the deck at that angle, "they've got something or someone of importance aboard and needed the room aft on the lower deck for either storage or passenger accommodations. At least they're under gunned; though I can't tell if those are larger bore than what we have. Most likely they have long guns for chasers. Let's see how far they will follow us before we run off."

"Can dat be safe? To let dem close on us like dis?" Beppe asked with incredulity in his tone.

Jez's smile was grim. "Nothing we do is safe out here Beppe, but I want some idea of where they are headed. If it is out to sea, we might still be able to take them if we can get behind and come up on the starboard side. There is a fort well up the coast of this peninsula that seems to get its income through Cuba, that possibly could be their next stop. I am hoping that is the case, for then there could be coin aboard as well as other supplies. If we can find a spot to let them go by, we might be able to come up on them quietly after dark and take them with a boarding party. There's enough coral reef out here that if they go up the coast they will likely slow down as night falls. They are riding rather low so they would be foolish not to. Even if they go on out to sea with the current, we'll be rid of them and can continue with our hunting. In any event I would rather have them before us than behind."

Beppe sighed and shook his head. "I wonder will I ever get used to dis life. But if dis what you wish for us to do Capitana, it will be what we do. What now your orders?" Archie had just joined them, catching part of the conversation.

"Men be ready to defend the tops Mum," he interjected and she nodded.

Jez took one more look at the following ship, then snapping shut the glass she said, "Hug the coast yet stay ahead of them. We will find some place—perhaps an inlet—to slip out of sight. I do not think we will strike anything here. If they come in too close though, *they* might. They probably know that." She turned to favor Beppe with a wolfish smile. "Night boardings are the most successful and we do have the pirogue. Darkness favors the predator more than the prey."

Her quartermaster sighed but then recalling their earlier adventure with *Sea Witch*, where *Revelation* had come in through the fog to take out the Spanish ship and help cripple the Portuguese caravel, he knew his captain understood her business.

"We will do it your way Capitana, for you are both bold and have much experience. Now let me get dis ship moving fast and perhaps we find another hiding place where we can let them pass by and den come in from behind."

The smaller ship they had sighted—which had initially appeared to be English built but was now flying a Bandera de Francia—began pulling well ahead of the galleon. Always somber and often unsmiling, Capitán Bartolomé Espósito y Serrano aboard the *Nueva España* knew full that these could still be pirates, many of whom often captured ships of another country and used certain flags as a ruse. Neither country's ships were to be trusted as also the Dutch were not. All had raided the Spanish ships and some colonies as pirates or privateers.

These who were assumed to be French now appeared to be heading toward the southwestern coastline, and while Captain Espósito felt they were too small to take on a fort, they would still bear watching. His entire crew was somewhat uneasy, for often pirate ships held many more men aboard than they appeared to. On this short trip from Cuba to St. Augustine, his own vessel was rather overloaded, so they were not making great speed. She was undermanned and definitely under-gunned, so they were not looking forward to a fight. Yet the smaller ship's tack taking them closer to the shoreline lead those aboard the wallowing Spanish galleon to believe that these strangers were more interested in establishing trade contact with the local savages, for most of what was down in this section were native people who were far from friendly.

If it was the French, they were likely looking to make contact with the natives and establish a trading post and perhaps a mission, none of which was Captain Espósito ship's concern. He had to get their load and passengers safely delivered as soon as possible, and there would likely be important dispatches to be carried back to Havana. From what they had been told, the native Indios were brutal butchers, so it was quite likely that all who went ashore from that French ship would lie dead by nightfall anyway. His orders were to head directly to St. Augustine where some maldito corsario Inglés had all but destroyed the settlement and presidio, even damaging the wooden fort. He was told that food and funds were critically low and plans for a new and far larger fortification were desperately needed.

The *Nueva España* had aboard engineers from Cuba and their instruments, their slave assistants, some workmen, copious food, some tobacco, sugar, and wine, along with several chests of silver reales and one of gold escudos to pay for additional slaves, putas, or workers who would be coming in soon as well.

Room for all the people they carried along with a special concealed amario—a cupboard area providing storage for the coinage—was in the cleared section of the gun deck. No one expected Spanish civilians to sleep in hammocks strung between cannons or down on the bare deck next to their slaves. As far as the dineros, there would be too much temptation for even the crew with that much currency aboard unless it was properly secured. Plus, it would be more properly hidden from pirates should they encounter anyone. Hearing that, of course the engineers insisted that their own very expensive tools and materials should also be stored in that narrow cupboard space, which meant things had to be moved around again to accommodate them. Captain Espósito had argued that down in the hold there was still plenty of room and much in the way of tools and supplies that would be needed for excavating and laying the foundation of this far more massive structure already, but those men would not be swayed. These were not things you simply rubbed the rust and rat shit off of before use, they argued. These finer tools must be kept dry and free of corrosion to be useful. The engineers had their way and the expensive tools they used would be stored with the coin chests, though well above the deck on a special shelf where they could not fall and suffer any damage.

Capitán Espósito had initially been irked when he was made to realize that they could not keep all the cannon aboard and have enough room for these alterations that allowed for both the passengers and this rather hefty cargo. It had proved to be simply a matter of properly balancing the load, so instead of offloading their guns, they jettisoned some ballast and then moved the demi-culverins down below to be used as ballast in the bottom of the hold, where at least his unused guns would not be sold to the highest bidder while he and his ship were away. The empty cannon carriages were stacked and tied down in front of the amario to disguise it after they finally had it filled and sealed into a section of bulkhead. This resourceful man had not moved up through the ranks by being foolish in believing that something left behind would remain in port very long. Especially not in busy Havana Harbor, where other ambitious men there were always making deals for their own benefit.

So, with all that refitting, they had gotten a later start than had been planned. At his orders they had piled on enough sail to move forward as rapidly as possible so that they could keep an eye on the French ship, yet it had proved to be able to move far faster than they could. By dusk the galleon's lookouts had lost sight of it.

With great caution they had rounded the tip of the Florida peninsula and headed up the eastern side, initially staying within the current, but there was no trace of the small brig. Capitán Espósito hoped that meant they had moved on—either out to sea or a stop somewhere inland. In any event there was no sign of them, neither sail nor lantern. Troubling perhaps, but being a wary man, he kept his ship in the deeper sea lane for now and hoped for the best.

He was only passingly familiar with the area, for *Nueva España* did not usually come this far north. They normally patrolled the area from South Eastern Cuba down to Puerto Rico and Hispaniola, keeping a close eye what came through the Windward, Mona, and Anegada Passages and down the Bahama Channel. They also cruised around Hispaniola to keep an eye on French Tortuga's notorious buccaneers and up to the Bahama Islands where piracy was also now well established and most of the population turned a blind eye to it. Unfortunately, he had been tapped for this particular trip when Havana had no one of their own to spare. Rumor had it that the infamous pirate king Henry Morgan was taking a fleet from Jamaica out to the Spanish Main soon and so many of the larger patrol ships had been sent ahead to watch for signs of that. The few remaining were charged with guarding the big Spanish island. Some were also watching closely the waters around Providencia, an island in an archipelago off the mainland *Nuevo Reino de Granada* where the pirate who had attacked St. Augustine had reportedly come from. That particular island had grown to be yet another haven for pirates and privateers.

"Capitán, the men want to know, do we proceed in the dark as planned or are we still hunting the Barco Francés? It is time for lighting the lanterns, sí?"

Espósito pursed his lips and rubbed his chin, making a rasping sound over his dark brown and tufted little beard and then twiddling the unwaxed and carefully trimmed ends of his mustache out of habit.

"I do believe it unwise to travel unlit in these waters," he said with a frown. "Have them light the stern and bow lanterns but make sure there are men in the tops well above them watching for signs of that ship coming back for us. Should they prove to be piratas, I would not assume that they would simply go off without engaging. Something about this situation feels wrong to me. We must be on our guard." As the other man went off to his duties, their Captain adjusted his baldric so that his sheathed sword would not drag and then made sure that none of his long-waving brown locks was caught beneath it. Settling the Cavalier hat he wore on his head at a properly rakish angle, he noted that the wind had turned the plume the wrong way and irritably snatched it off and straightened everything out once more. He was not as much a fop as someone who could not stand disorder of any kind, at least not when he still had time to think about it. So far, this entire short voyage had been nothing but one vexation after another.

He captained his ship with the same attention to detail. It bothered the devil out of him how slow they were running and how sloppily it sailed, but it was overloaded and he himself had insisted on keeping the guns aboard.

Thankfully this trip was relatively short. As he crisply strode down and around the upper decks on his evening pass, he glanced up at the set of the sails, the tautness of halyards or braces, and around at how lines were coiled. He insisted on a few adjustments but otherwise, found all was primarily as well as it could be. At every opportunity Captain Espósito took one more good look around the area with the long glass but it was quite dark by then, so little could be seen. He then turned the deck over to one of his deck officers and headed down to his cabin for a late dinner and a chance to enjoy an extra glass of fine Madeira while he wrote in his log about their day.

With the stern windows still open, the cabin was warm but not airless, the food was adequate if plain, and the Madeira much to his liking—not too sweet or too dry. He was scratching away in flowing script with the inked quill when the call came from above.

"*Capitán, ¡nos persiguen!*"

Revelation had made very good time sailing up the coast. Right before it got dark, they spotted an opening to a large bay. Much of the water within was shallow due to reefs, sandbars, and grass flats, plus there were small cays. It took some careful maneuvering as the sun began to set to get a ship even as shallow drafted as the brig rigged pinnace within.

Eventually they found a relatively hospitable spot behind one narrow end of a large sandy cay that would effectively hide the ship while giving it quick access again to the deep water inlet. There was no obvious settlement nearby, so they tied up both bow and stern behind a screen of mangrove and palms, which with reefed topsails kept them in the lee of the wind.

While they waited for nightfall and the small coastal galleon to pass, it was time to propose their options to her lads. While these fellows were originally English Navy and used to blindly following orders, pirate vessels did not operate that way, and Jez was no tyrant captain. Her crew had a chance to vote on whether they would take on what was normally a well-armed vessel with an experienced crew like that coastal galleon or pass on it and look for something else. After all, they were trusting her instincts and experience in choosing potential prizes and pirating was always a dangerous business.

"No whistles or bells but pass the word around to call all the men quietly on deck. Get someone to stir up a barrel of bumbo. Only one mug each for now. I need to speak to the entire crew—even the youngsters," Jez told Beppe. "And I don't want them all drunk."

"It will be done Capitana," he promised and quietly informed the entire crew. Within minutes they were assembled on the weather deck. Jez strode amidst them all where she would be heard without shouting, dressed in her normal tar-stained canvas slops, baggy linen shirt, and barefoot with her long, dark shining hair plaited in multiple braids tipped with colorful beads. Hands on slender hips, she glanced around and smiled.

"Lads, you're likely not used to this, but on a pirate ship, all get a vote before we take any action that is not necessary for defense reasons. So, I want to lay this out for you to think over, though we must decide quickly and quietly." She stopped a moment to gather her thoughts and let the surprised muttering end before going on.

"That ship we outpaced appears to be one of the smaller Spanish coastal patrol galleons. I want to impress on all of you that the Spanish down here are very capable enemies and so even their sailors will fight—plus they often have marines aboard. Now this ship is unusual because it is showing only half its gun deck ports are operational and all of those are toward the fore. That suggests to me that they had to remove some cannon to make room for something else they're carrying, which could be passengers, extra cargo, or a combination of both. We've already noted, by the way they are sailing, that they are not in good balance. The fact that we outran them says a lot too. They are hauling some heavy items aboard. I would like to know what that might be."

Again she paused as men were sharing things they had noticed with one another other. Beppe gave them all a stern glance and they quieted down so Jez could go on.

"What I propose is that we watch for them to pass and then get in behind them to see if we can take them now that it's dark. They could be heading out to sea, but I rather suspect they might be following the coast to a fort I've seen farther up on the Florida Peninsula. As I recall it was behind some sort of barrier island. That could well be the destination, and if they came from the big Spanish island of Cuba, they might have payrolls and other coins in silver and possibly gold. They're also likely to have food, rum, wine, or other goods aboard that the fort asked for. Perhaps passengers as well—some of whom might be wealthy. If we can take them at night without a lot of damage or casualties on our end and cripple their ship we'll take a quick run back to Tortuga with whatever we have. Some portion of that plunder will be ours to keep, so when we go out again, we'll head south next and see what we can find down that way."

She continued speaking as the muttering began again, cutting them off from speculating, for time was against them.

"Now I want to stress to you all that there is great risk involved. Some of us will likely be injured or possibly killed. Such risk is part of any sailor's life, as I'm sure you all know—it's doubly so for pirates. Yet the choice is yours this time: Do we pursue this or not? You have a few minutes to think it over, then I want a quiet chorus of ayes and then nays. Also, all will be heard, and none should fear to voice his opinion, for no man aboard my ship will be chastised or shunned for how he votes—that lads *is* an order."

"Have someone let me know what the consensus is," Jez said to Beppe before she headed down to her cabin to peruse charts and await the outcome, her crew parting to let her pass through.

It did not take long, for these men had been treated far better under Captain Johnston than they'd ever been in the previous merchant ships or navies they had served in. There *were* a few nays, but the majority were in favor, and when Archie brought the news, Jez felt closer to her lads than ever before.

"All right then!" she said with great enthusiasm, getting to her feet. "Tell Beppe one more mug of bumbo for all, then get some men out there on the cay to keep watch and bring word back. Have others form potential gun crews. Warn all of our lads that we need to make ready to sail at a moment's notice."

Once Jez was back on deck there was a waxing gibbous moon so the night would be fairly bright. Timing would be everything in making a successful boarding. Recalling how in the keys Pakke had been sent out to climb a tree to watch for ships coming by, Jez had Beppe send one of the smaller, more agile men who could be trusted to keep watch out to the point of the cay with a view of the open water. There would be enough light tonight to catch sight of oncoming sails before any ship was in full sight. Two other men accompanied the one in the tree and were stationed down on the ground at intervals to bring word back quickly if anything was spotted. All were armed, for they did not know this land.

"No shouting, bell ringing, or piping!" she warned Beppe yet again, for those English Navy habits seemed to be ingrained. "I want that passed on because sound carries far at night. Pulling this off greatly depends on stealth." She already had Jengo consulting with Archie about choosing men to be ready as a boarding party, for they would heading out in the pirogue once they were close behind the Spanish ship and had crippled her in a way that if all went well, Jez knew would leave her dead adrift in the water. As captain, of course she'd be joining that boarding party too.

The call finally came a couple hours before midnight—much later than she had expected. Jez had retired to her cabin to get some rest, but she was a little apprehensive about this potential encounter, so it took her some time to settle down. She had finally drifted off into a sound slumber when there was a flurry of knocking that woke her up. A familiar low rumbling voice said from the door, "Jez, the Spanish ship be coming up in the channel, still well out to sea but she not moving too fast."

Wide awake immediately, Jez exploded out of her bunk. She yanked on her boots, stowed her hidden knife in the right one, and then grabbed her head scarf. She deftly tied that on over her long beaded braids so that all hung down in back where nothing would obscure her view. She was out the door in moments.

"They're positive this is the one we saw earlier Jengo?" she queried in a quiet tone and the big man nodded as she vaulted up the nearest ladder right behind him. He also kept his voice low.

"Yeah, they be sure. Well lit up she be and just poke along. 'Wallowing' is what the man who seen it say when I question him, he make motions like an old donkey carry a big pack. That mean they be overloaded or no good balance. I thinkin' it because they still have some bigger bore guns, but all that weight be forward. Even if you ballast on other end to level it, ship don't sail right in a runnin' sea when somethin' heavy is close to top, something else way below."

"To remove guns like that, they must have needed the lower deck space for something important," Jez said in a speculative tone as they stood together just below the quarterdeck. "That also means they'll have to come about far slower as well, because of that tall aftercastle with the poop deck. Otherwise, they risk twisting the frame and opening seams underwater. You know Jengo, I like these odds better all the time," she said with a wolfish grin.

"Me too." He looked up and around them. "Your crew, they raising sail already and untie to leave. I thought you need be told first."

She looked up at the sky, where she could make it out between freshening sails. "Every minute counts and the moon will set soon, so Beppe knows we need to cast off quickly to make it safely out of here," she told him in a reassuring tone. "A lot of this bay is low water, and we don't want to get stuck on a sandbar or founder on a reef. Archie would have had men in the tops already anyway—this bunch knows their sailing business. If you see Paddy, tell him I said to get gun crews together again, we'll at least need men on those long bore fores right away in case we have to fire a warning shot as we close in. Hopefully it won't come to broadsides. I have to speak with Beppe and the helmsman, but then I've got to get ready to lead the boarding party. We'll want you with us as well—most of my lads have only boarded as pirates once and that was no warship, nor was it heavily guarded. A Spanish galleon captain will surely want to make a stand against us."

"Then we will fight back!" Jengo said with his usual enthusiasm. "I be ready now," he added indicating the well-used baldric with its tarnished silver buckle crossing his stained linen shirt, for he had two pistols, and a knife tucked into it along with powder and shot. He'd also had his favorite cutlass in a frog hanging off his belt, which was buckled over worn black and tan striped breeches.

Jengo went on. "I already know which men to take. They just need time to arm up," the burly, dark skinned man said with a toothy grin. "Archie have man to take care o' arming them. You and me Jez, we can handle this."

"That's why I'm glad to have you aboard again, matey," she said with feeling and a relieved smile, giving Jengo a back slap that got her a wink before he pounded away down the weather deck toward the forecastle, where below were the men he and Archie had chosen as potential boarders. The cockney man would remain aboard to see to the those on the sails and the few they had who could aim a musket from above.

Jez headed up to the quarterdeck. She needed to quickly touch base with whoever had the wheel as well as Beppe before she finished her own preparations. She made her instructions fast and simple for she had more preparations of her own to attend to before they closed on the Spanish ship. Plus, she wanted time to talk to those who would be boarding.

"Once out of this bay we want to catch up to them yet remain well enough behind their aft chasers' gun range so as not to take a direct hit," she explained to Beppe and the helmsman. "We likely can't get close enough for a shot of our own unless we can somehow get around them on the weather side and steal some wind. We still need to stay well behind their operating gunports, which all seem to be toward the foredeck. Those big bore guns don't move that far to the sides, so that should be safe enough for us if we're careful. Because of the lack of cannon, they likely have marines in the tops and swivel guns on the gunwales, so we will take some raking fire. We just need to have our lads use canister loads to clear the decks and maybe some bar or chain to take down sails or yards, maybe a mast if we can manage that."

"Dis all be done, no worry Capitana," Beppe said and she nodded at him and hustled off. Already it was growing darker, but they had rounded the end of the cay and were in the narrow channel where they'd come into the bay.

Other than procuring and carefully cradling a lit slow match stub, Jez headed directly back to her cabin. She used that to light her gimbal lamp and then dunked it into her tiny basin of wash water to put out the smoldering tip. As pirate captain, she had to lead the boarding party to show them how bold she was, and she needed to look the part of the successful yet fearsome foe. She needed some light in order to line some dark kohl around her eyes to make herself look dangerous and she added a bit of rouge to her lips, making the cut lip scar stand out. Jez also grabbed her hat and favorite hanger in its sheath along with a brace of loaded pistols.

Securing the handguns in reach meant having to tighten up the sash so they'd stay in place. Jez realized she should acquire one of those baldrics like Jengo had—though something new and far fancier to show off her status. She would try to buy one somewhere once they were back in port. In the meantime, she doubled the cloth around her narrow waist, making it tight enough to hold everything in place and then buckled the belt over it with her sheathed blade on the left for a quick cross draw.

Pistols had to be properly stowed because she'd likely be climbing up the side of the ship they were boarding, perhaps even while being shot at, so those went securely into the doubled sash underneath the belt. Jez always had a knife in her boot and these days another longer one sheathed on her right hip opposite the hanger sheathed on her left. You couldn't have too many weapons on you for a boarding, especially in what could potentially be a difficult encounter with well experienced fighting men.

With one last glance in her looking glass, she darkened the kohl even more. Once she was satisfied, she was dressed properly to appear to be a fierce and successful pirate captain, it was time to go topside. Jez could feel *Revelation* heeling to larboard to make the turn out to sea, so they had already exited the channel they'd come in by. No bottoming out then—that was a relief! She blew out the lantern and headed back up onto the quarter deck. Beppe met her there.

"Capitana, de Spagnola ship has already pass by. Dey mebbe half a glass somewhere ahead. Dey make up de time with full sails on."

"So shall we Beppe. Bring her around with a full set and run up the French jack for now. I've still got to get us a *Joli Rouge* sewn up so that will have to do."

Beppe was already issuing orders for additional sails as she headed toward the forecastle to see what was up with the men who would be boarding. Halfway there Jez could hear the snap of sails filling overhead as they were clewed in place along with the creak of bulkheads and wind sawing through the various lines and hawsers. She felt *Revelation* come around beneath them and picking up speed. She had just reached the forecastle ladder when someone up in the foremast top shouted, "Ship ho, moving away to north, nor'east!"

"Is it the galleon?" she hollered back up and it took him a moment to confirm.

"It appears so Ma'am," he said with some certainty. "Big fancy aftcastle and she's yawing quite a bit. They must have seen us, they've full sails up now, and close reached."

"Aye, they've seen us all right. Keep piling on those sails!" she bellowed back and men along the way passed the word as they made the changes necessary. Yard extensions were quickly added for upper stunsails and additional canvas billowed and snapped as all were adjusted for angle until they caught the wind well. *Revelation* picked up speed, cutting through the waves like a hunting barracuda. Jez knew they could not afford to let this one get away, there had to be something of great worth aboard for them not to come about and take a stand.

So, the chase was on! Jengo joined Jez on the foredeck.

"They run scared now," he said grinning and she agreed with a nod.

"I would too with such an unbalanced ship. As I recall, there's not much down here along the coast but reefs and open land—some scattered islands or cays. Maybe an inlet, but I cannot say for sure. I just don't want them heading out to sea on us."

"They won't get far," he said with a sneer that showed gold teeth. "One big wave or gust gonna throw them 'round with the way they fight at the helm with full sails on. We get them yet!"

"I know we will," Jez agreed.

Once well out in the ocean strait again, with the moon well up and the water still fast, they could easily make out the elaborately figured and painted stern castle of the small galleon up ahead. The Spanish still had lanterns lit fore and aft, probably not trusting that they'd be able to judge the water or be seen by other ships without them. That told Jez and Jengo that this ship had not regularly sailed this far north—at least not under the current captain and crew. Lanterns were a big mistake if you wanted to move off from a potential aggressor without being seen, although with no fog and decent moonlight this night, it might not have mattered much.

Jezebel Johnston was sure now that this captain was not as seasoned as some she had dealt with. That was certainly a plus in her favor!

Aboard lumbering *Nueva España*, while they were full under sail with a broad reach and fast following sea, they were barely making seven knots, and the ship was yawing terribly. The problem was those cannons down in the ballast area. Unlike square cut stones, they were long, rounded, and tapered so even with the projecting trunnions on either side of the barrel that normally held them in the wooden carriage, they were still prone to shifting as the ship turned or heeled. Men were down there now trying to move them into a better position so they could be properly fixed in place, but those guns were extremely heavy, and the reeking bilge scum had to be pumped out before anyone could see what they were doing or get a proper idea of how to reposition them. The captain's plan had depended on the weight of the cannons alone to keep them in place, for they had not had time to properly secure them before leaving Havana. That oversight was now costing them too much in the way of speed as well as maneuverability. Yet they had been forced to leave the Cuban harbor on the timetable of those in St. Augustine who were in desperate need of the supplies, building experts, tools, and funding they had aboard. In Havana it had been deemed a short trip north that should have been quite feasible.

Yet now these malditos piratas had shown up once again! This time they were *behind* his ship and gaining rapidly. Without looking down at their position in the water Capitán Espósito could feel the lack of balance through the abnormal heaving of the deck beneath his feet. Because the trade wind off the ocean had picked up there were now swells coming from starboard, so he stood clutching the stern rail of the poop deck with his left hand as he raised his mahogany and brass telescopio to his right eye once more. He had to let go the rail and back up to be safe from being thrown off balance while adjusting it, but then began swearing under his breath. Even with barely enough moonlight to make out the smaller ship he could tell that it also was running full sails. It was far closer than first reported and taking a weather tack to cut them off from the wind as much as possible.

He snapped shut his expanded glass for the fifth time since he had learned they were being followed, and continued barking orders to his helm and the oficial de intendencia for those in the sails. Men around him scrambled to obey, for whatever good it would do now.

It was that same Francés brig once again! Espósito shook a gloved fist at it in anger. He had not wanted this assignment—not with his normally graceful ship being overloaded, stripped of guns, and now sailing so awkwardly. He was tempted to toss some of those so-important building materials and tools overboard, but if there was an inquiry and they found out he had kept his inactive cannon in lieu of proper ballast, he'd be removed from command, perhaps go to prison, or be brought before an inquisitor on some trumped up charges. He would certainly lose any land claims here in New Spain and his already financially struggling parents back home in Segovia might be turned out into the street. If any of that came to pass and he somehow managed to be acquitted, his reputation would still be tainted by the inquiry. No decent woman of fine lineage with a dowry would have him for a husband regardless of why he had done so—and he still a quite handsome man of good breeding in his early middle years. No, it was far better to fight and be wounded or die a hero aboard. Perhaps then his family might receive some compensation.

Ah, but Bartolomé Espósito y Serrano did not wish to die. He had a plan, but it would take some convincing of his men to carry out.

"Alejandro!" he called to his master mate. "Run up the bandera blanca." The man who was his dependable second in command gave him a shocked look, knowing the crew would never agree.

"Oh, mi Capitán, por favor, excuse my questioning this order," the older, far more experienced sailor pleaded in a low voice as he tentatively approached, "but we should not do this with what we have hidden away below. The piratas will swarm aboard and threaten to kill someone, and then there will be panic. Most likely the engineers will speak of it to save their own lives. Of course such contemptible hombres brutales as piratas will kill us all anyway!" In the flickering lantern light Alejandro's swarthy features had gone pale and he appeared aghast over the situation they were in. "It is better to die in battle than to surrender all."

Espósito was furious with that reply! "You think I am a coward who would give up so easily!" he roared at the man, gesticulating wildly and gaining the attention of others around them. "No, you estúpido, we are moving too slowly to defend ourselves in the usual manner! So, they will capture us, killing many and torturing men for information regardless if we fight or not. But piratas always send a party aboard with their own capitán, who wants to swagger before his men. So, we will only pretend to surrender; a ruse to get them to bring up their ship and divide their men. It must be close enough that at my command we rake their deck with fire from some of our infantería de marina hidden in the tops before we blow a hole in their hull, and then we will successfully kill them all. When we are triumphant, we will move on again and you will all have stories to tell the senoritas in the tabernas when we get back to Santo Domingo, eh?" Espósito looked around his dark eyes glowing. "This you see," he said, tapping his head, "is how you use strategy to overcome an enemy."

"Quite clever indeed," Alejandro answered rather drily, for he doubted very much the pirates approaching would be so easily fooled. Yet it was worth trying. "It will be done as you wish Capitán," he added while turning away to issue orders.

Revelation was drawing close enough now that they could make out some details of the small galleon's fancy stern gallery. It wasn't as elaborate as the

"This, you see, is how you use strategy to overcome an enemy."

larger ships that were used for trade, but from what could be seen in the Spanish vessel's onboard lantern light showed that it had its share of painted carvings and gold leaf. Jez noted right away the poop deck's gun ports were open and that those chasers had been run out, indicating that they would retaliate at any show of aggression. The men she had spoken with who had watched the Spanish ship pass by said they noted no sign of weather deck cannons other than those up front, and that now all the lower gun deck gun ports were closed. That was likely against slop from the increased wave action and the ship's rather lurching progress. They would be taking on water through those ports—at least on the starboard side—with the way she was riding so low in the water and the occasional angle of pitch and yaw.

Even these smaller galleons were built for stability so there had to be an unusual source of unbalance—either in the hold or with the ballast below. Maybe they had a leak where a bad seam had sprung or a patch let go? Yet crews would be on the pumps while anything like that would have been fixed. In any event, this was definitely something a pirate could take advantage of.

All this Jez discussed with Beppe, Archie, Paddy, and Jengo, though right up on the quarterdeck where the rest of the crew could see them and they'd certainly be overheard. There were no secrets on her ship!

"We have a good chance of taking them if we can cripple their ability to sail," she said. "The trick is to do it fast and without unnecessarily endangering our ship and crew or damaging their ship so much it founders. I have an idea, but I want to run it by you fellows first."

She took a deep breath before continuing. This was something Jez had been mulling over for a few hours, based on previous experiences but it was not without great risk.

"Judging from the lack of freeboard and the sluggish way she responds along with the listing, they're grossly overloaded and out of balance. Yet if you've noticed, they don't seem very eager to jettison any cargo to level her off and either make up speed to move faster or come around at us. So, I still say there has to be something of great importance aboard." There was general agreement. "For now let us steal what we can of their wind then take out some of their sails as they slow down, but we have to do it fast, before they dare run out the guns they have. Then if we can get a good low shot at the stern of that ship Paddy," she caught her head gunner's eye, "we might be able to cripple their rudder. I have seen that done before; they are always a gudgeon and pintle setup that becomes useless once they're blasted away." Beppe nodded thoughtfully at that, and Jengo smiled broadly, because Jez had learned so much. "Even taking out the top fastener or blowing off a good part of the actual rudder will keep them from sailing off out to sea on us or being able to effectively turn and fire."

She turned to Paddy and asked, "Can you do that at close range with one of our fore guns without sinking them?"

He cocked his head and took a deep breath. "Aye, I can surely hit somethin' Mum, but even close up, in this chop it's powerful hard to be so precisely accurate. We'd be likely to blow a hole in the stern and then she takes on water and upends. Be it worth the chance we hit them wrong, or they manage to get us?"

Jez frowned and thought that over. "What if we come in at an angle with something small—a case load maybe? Hit them from the side after raking their sails? We might just cripple them."

"What about de rail guns?" Beppe asked. "We have some aboard, dey most used for signal and to arm de long boat we had. We can set dem up quick and den shoot more accurate with dat at such close range."

Paddy's eyes lit up and he slapped his forehead. "Aye, I clean forgot about them! T'would be far easier to line up a true aim with those. Might take more than one shot to cripple her rudder, but I'm positive we can hit it with that without blowing her arse to hell in the process."

"Can you get enough of a hit to penetrate it though?" Jez brusquely asked Paddy, for galleon rudders were thick. Time was of the essence, for they were starting to close in on the larger ship from their larboard side, edging toward her starboard.

"With me eyes closed and a hand tied behind me back mum. I got good fellas on the gun crews, but this be something I'm best doing meself. I got it figured already." He tapped his right temple with a tarry forefinger.

"Make ready to cripple them then," Jez said in an upbeat tone while stifling a sigh of relief, for a captain could never sound uneasy about leading men into battle.

This was what was good about pirating, having crew members with a background in a particular area who were now used to thinking for themselves rather than just taking orders from above. "Step lively lads, we're close to engaging," she quipped with a wicked grin. "Be watchful above for us, they likely have armed marines aboard. Pick off any you see once we're in range. Let's rake those sails as soon as we're close enough. I want to knock any armed men down, there's bound to be some in the fighting tops and the crow's nest if we can reach it. Their masts are taller than ours, they'll have the advantage of shooting down at our top decks. If we can quickly drop rigging and sails all along the deck and down her sides, that should foul her further. Then we shall stop all her forward movement so we can climb aboard maties."

Revelation's crew, having been regular English Navy, knew what to do before a battle. Men had already been hustling about their business. Her decks were sanded for traction and to soak up blood, the safety nets were out, and extra ropes, line, yarn, and spars had been brought up from the orlop area below for quick repairs. On the gun deck below, hammocks were cleared and sand in buckets holding lengths of slow match ready to be ignited were waiting. All the racks against the sides between the guns were filled with iron balls or other ordnance. The banked coals in the galley were mostly out; just a potful left covered in the oven in case more slow matches for the guns were needed to be lit. The big prep table and the one the crewmen ate at were completely cleared for treating the wounded.

On the top decks, the fore cannons were now run out, once the tompions were removed they had been loaded. Paddy and his boys brought up six swivel guns; four were small but two were actually mini cannons. The petite quartet were lined up two each side on the gunnels as anti-personnel weapons to sweep the decks of the galleon of potential combatants. The mini cannons Paddy had up on the quarterdeck rail on each side where he could get a good downward shot at that rudder—or anything else that needed pinpoint accuracy at close range with a load that would be sufficient enough to do some local damage.

Archie had three men good with muskets stationed on their own top platforms. Jengo had his boarders assembled as well, though it was not certain now if they'd need the pirogue because it looked as if they might just throw grapples with line to pull the ships together, lay down some heavy boards for crossing, and swarm over. He made sure boarding pikes and axes along with cutlasses were readily available and there was heavy planking nearby to be laid. Now all they had to do was close in, cripple her, and then the takeover rout would begin.

It was a surprise when a white flag went up on the Spanish ship. Men aboard *Revelation* cheered. Jez and Jengo, who had been discussing the potential boarding, were not so easily thrilled.

"I don' like this Jez. They surrender too quick," Jengo said with a scowl that made his dark face appear almost demonic in the waning moonlight. "Could be trap."

"I was thinking the same thing," Jez said with a frown. "We will proceed with caution, but I don't want to be caught by surprise. No quarter. We shoot anyone who appears aggressive."

"You damn right!" Jengo said. "They keep the hands up and big guns inside or we blow them away." Men amongst the boarders were watching them now, most coping with pre-battle nerves, some now looking at the ship they were closing on in bewilderment or disbelief. These were men chosen because they had some experience in shipboard fighting situations in their previous naval posts, for the packet ship that *Revelation* used to be seldom had to engage. All of them trusted Captain Johnston, but if something made her and this well experienced Negro pirate they had come to trust suspicious, they knew they would need to be extra wary as well.

"Hopefully it won't come to that," Jezebel Johnston said in a lighter, more offhand tone while noting that her men were becoming restive, though her unease heightened as they closed in. Something here just felt... *wrong*.

CHAPTER EIGHT

Aboard *Nueva España* some very subtle but crucial changes had been made. All civilians had been banished down to the hold for their own safety, though they had been given blades if it became necessary to defend themselves. Men who were not needed on the remaining big guns or in the tops had been quietly arming up for shipboard conflict. Spanish warships that patrolled the Caribbean area were known to carry large crews in case of running across such a threat. Capitán Bartolomé Espósito y Serrano had insisted on keeping his entire company aboard for that reason—these waters were now brimming with pirate vessels.

The area they normally cruised through had long been a hotbed of old-time buccaneers but now there were many younger freebooters who were especially bloodthirsty. Hispaniola had been recently attacked by French pirates from Tortuga and the smaller three-masted Spanish coastal galleon's young captain had expressed a desire to be part of the retaliation force that bombarded Tortuga's harbor at night. To his distaste Espósito had been issued other orders and was sent up to Havana to deliver this cargo along with the civil engineers to St. Augustine.

The irony that he was now facing a pirate attack of his own was not lost on him as they made ready to engage. They had moved a couple of the lighter guns around, which had caused the ship to become additionally hard to steer but put some firepower in a much more useful position. Those guns were now loaded and waiting, yet their ports remained closed—for now. With a change in the tackle that handled them, either port could be very quickly opened and the gun run out to be fired into the very hull of the pirate ship, hopefully crippling but not outright sinking her. It would take perfect timing, but it was their best chance of surviving this encounter.

Espósito had thought his plan of action out carefully. These piratas might well be from Tortuga, for they were still boldly flaunting a bandera Francesa. It would not take long to sail up this far. It would be a boon for his career should he kill most of them and perhaps capture a few such as their capitán for interrogation before they were hanged—even better if he managed to take their trim little ship without sinking it and put a prize crew aboard to sail it back to Havana. That would certainly give his more well-connected detractors something to think about!

He watched closely but with grim satisfaction the pirate ship approaching them now as the *bandera blanca de rendición* had been raised. That was a ruse of course; they just needed this ship which was now actively chasing them to be very close for what he had in mind.

"*Puestos de batalla!*" he called out in a softly voiced tone of command; an order to be repeated quietly from man-to-man all up and down the decks as the French pirate ship began to steal their wind. Already his ship's lower sails were losing their trim and beginning to sag.

"*Aquí vienen ellos,*" he whispered to the man stationed at his side as he fiddled with the hailing trumpet. Continuing in soft voiced Castilian he said, "*Tell the gunners that when they hear me address the piratas that they need to stand ready. When I welcome them aboard, then they are to run out just the gun that was just placed on the starboard quarter, light it immediately, and shoot a hole at their waterline. Then we take out their masts if necessary. Ve rápido ahora!*"

The man saluted and barreled off immediately as ordered, shoving men out of his way before rushing down the ladder to the gun deck two steps at a time.

As the neat little square rigged brig drew closer, everyone aboard *Nueva España* tensed and made ready for the bloodbath to come, for she was well enough gunned to do some damage and the pirate crew appeared capable.

"Capitana, something is no right here." Beppe was shaking his head as he spoke in a worried tone while Jez made ready to board. "Dese Spagnoli, we know dey fight hard and not give up so easy. Is trick I am sure. Please to be careful."

"Always," she reassured him while keeping a watchful eye on the larger ship they were cautiously approaching. Jez had her own misgivings as well, but she would not allow the crew to witness any hesitation on her part. Pirate or navy man, sailors always looked up to their captain for direction and encouragement. She had gotten them into this, she'd get them out as well, as safely as possible while facing the same dangers they would.

"Ready on the guns," she bellowed, more for sobering effect than because the lads needed her to tell them their business. They were just coming abreast the Spanish ship's starboard aft quarter when she caught the hint of a flickering glow coming from the last of the covered apertures on the galleon's gun deck. That light told her the port was not securely fastened shut and that someone was down there attending to something near that gunport—which was quite suspicious. The Spanish ship had a distinctive lean to starboard now, perhaps they had repositioned a gun?

"Jez, I see light–!" Jengo began because he had noted that hint of illumination as well, but he was cut off and had to duck and retreat when shots began to rain down from the galleon's fighting tops. Spanish marines shooting matchlocks were up there!

All was suddenly chaos aboard *Revelation*. Several men on her weather deck yelped as shots whizzed by or hit close enough to throw long wood splinters near where they had been working. Several were hit by those, they were painful and could easily take out an eye. One of the boarders in Jez's group, an older man with a decided limp couldn't get out of the way fast enough and he screamed and collapsed after being badly hit by a musket ball that was dead on shot from the galleon's mainmast fighting top. He went down squirming and kicking, clutching his red gushing midsection with eyes already rolling white until he suddenly lay still. Two of his companions dragged his bloody, contorted body off to one side.

Archie had three men who shot well up on their own narrow platforms and Jez ordered them to take aim at the Spanish marines, who unfortunately were wearing chest armor and helmets. These men of New Spain's Coastal Patrol outnumbered her sharpshooters at least five to one to one and so could stagger their shots to allow their partner to reload. The Spaniards were well-trained and experienced, so all were skilled marksmen. Yet their having fired first gave the pirate ship's musketeers one slight advantage, for while they could not always see the flash, their enemies' positions were marked by the twin spumes of smoke which indicated where each man was stationed. Those long, low set rectangular square rigged sails on the galleon's forward and main masts were angled far enough away to catch the wind so were impossible to hide behind. With Jez's ship on the weather side, *Revelation*'s smaller, more square billowing tops hid well the three gunners who fired back and then immediately ducked around the other side of the mast to reload. They only managed to hit one of the Spanish sharpshooters, though it was in the thigh, which fountained blood spray. He immediately dropped his weapon and grabbed at it, ripping off the strap of his powder flask to tie it off while his partner shot, but then he was hit again. After a long, loud outcry that sounded like a prayer he fell over backwards to drop like a sack of meal to the deck below, hitting it with a shuddering thud.

The smaller ship's gunners also took out some common sailors who were frantically adjusting yards and clewing sails and so made good targets. The less men they had in the tops, the slower that galleon would come around.

"Sails tack away; helm take us out a bit and then come back 'round before them quickly so we can put a shot right across their bow," Jez roared above the din and it was repeated down the decks.

Paddy meanwhile had barked orders to men on the larboard swivel guns. As *Revelation* began to pull off, they peppered the galleon's poop deck, quarterdeck, and waist with grapeshot. Fortunately the young powder monkeys had left them plenty of canisters of shot and extra mug-shaped chambers filled with black powder bags in the gunnel racks to use. That did nothing to discourage those well above in the galleon's tops, but it cleared the deck of potential sailors and marines below.

Jez turned to Jengo and the remainder of the boarding party. "These sneaky bastards meant to shoot a hole in our side once we were close enough!" she snarled as that last starboard gunport on the galleon suddenly flew open and a cannon was quickly run out, though to no avail with well-trimmed *Revelation* now veering off. The galleon's desperate downward shot plunked into the sea just out of range and to aft on the brig-rigged pinnace's larboard side. "This was a desperation ruse—so you can bet that they do have something extremely valuable or important aboard. We can maneuver faster than they can lumber into a turn, so we'll circle them and take out whatever we can to slow them down to a crawl without sinking her. Then we board. I want to take these tricksy arseholes down a peg or two before this is over."

Capitán Espósito furiously cursed over his ill luck. Somehow these piratas had figured out his ruse of drawing them close with the white flag of surrender in order to shoot a hole in their larboard side. Had that succeeded, he assumed that a goodly number of the pirate crew would have been sent below to deal with the incoming seawater, which would make maneuvering slower and cut down on the amount of men manning sails or their guns. Then his infantería de marina sharpshooters and a few tossed grenados with gravel and metal filings packed within would suffice to complicate things on their deck as *Nueva España* ponderously came around to aim his vessel's long reach stern chasers for taking out the pirate vessel's masts. At such short range, that would have hit at least one of their masts, dragging sails and rigging down. The men aboard the pirate navío would still beso busy pumping out incoming seawater and patching the hole in their side to keep their ship from foundering that with sails and mast falling and dragging as well, they'd not be able to run off, evening the odds between them.

All this had been his ingenious plan; but like most of his countrymen asea, he had a superior attitude of his own crew's prowess and a dim view of such murderous rabble as these. Unfortunately, his ship had lost the element of surprise when someone aboard the other ship must have grown suspicious for they began to tack away. His abrupt order was given to open fire but the cannon they had hastily relocated proved difficult to adjust and his rail gunners were being picked off. So, it was primarily the marines in the tops who were defending them. Alas... it was far too late now for second thoughts, as the French ship was beginning a circuitous turn to cut them off.

In spite of his frustration, Espósito had to admire their wariness. They must have a very experienced and skillful captain. There was no time left to abandon his cargo and sail away without being hit. His mind was made up; they would stand their ground and engage, for if he did not do so and managed to be spared after surrendering, he would be relieved of his command and branded a traitor. To face an honorable death in battle was far more desirable than a firing squad. Yet should they somehow survive and win the upper hand, it would send a message that *his* ship under *his* command would not be so easily overwhelmed, and that the Spanish were still the masters of all the Caribbean island waters. That at least would be to his benefit.

"*Atención a todos!*" he called out in a ringing tone as the French pirate ship to began pull ahead and started coming around at them. "We are now under attack, and we will fight these piratas to the death. Man your stations and be brave; let us make España proud!"

He noted that there was an undercurrent of cursing and prayers aboard, but his men were well trained and hurried to their stations, most now armed. Some were busy hoving to, others manned the forward cannons. As the smaller pirate ship bore down on them in the darkness, her own fore guns run out, they prepared to engage in a stationary battle.

"They gonna fight," Jengo said with a sigh that quickly turned into a toothy, admiring smile. "Even though they can barely move the ship. I think that take big ballocks."

Jez frowned—she would have preferred they surrender. "Then we'll have to beat the damn fight out of them as quickly as possible. You never know who else is lingering on this coast. I want to be out of here by dawn." A secondary plan had already suggested itself to her.

"Dunno if we can move their cargo that fast Jez," Jengo continued in a low voiced rumble, "they got somethin' heavy aboard. Could take time to unload."

"I'll worry about that later," she retorted brusquely as she hurried off to issue new commands. Jez needed to quickly get everyone set up. She sent a swift lad pounding back toward the stern to let Beppe know the new heading without depending on men to shout it down the line. Then in a loud voice, in order to be heard over the creaking of timbers and snap of sails overhead, Jez issued a specific order to the front gunners.

"We'll be coming around sharply shortly lads, for at this range they seem to have nothing but their fores to take us with. Load them with whatever will take out masts and sails and make ready to open fire on my command." As *Revelation* heeled abruptly before their actual turn began, a disgruntled Paddy had joined her, his thin, frowning, sunburned face wearing a puzzled and somewhat frustrated expression. She waved him to silence and tersely explained her idea.

"The situation has changed, but we'll still take out their rudder later, before we leave so they won't follow us. Right now, we're close enough to stop them from advancing—which they can still manage in this current. Their fore cannon are longer and larger than ours, so head-on, they have the range advantage. Because they're riding low in the water, they could leave those fores as is and manage to blow a hole in our prow or elevate them and skip one across our foredeck. Maybe take out our bowsprit to foul us. Any of those actions could do a lot of damage and slow us down, giving them time to reload."

"Beggin' pardon Mum," Paddy said brusquely, "but they might well open a starboard gunport and blow us t'hell an'ways, see'in' as our powder room be up front. Those first two ports be jist above bein' awash—so iffen t'was me o'er there, I'd chance it."

Jez nodded but went on in a rapidly spoken explanation. "As would I, but with our speed and the moon setting, I'm betting they can't get a starboard crew on those foredeck area guns in time to have them loaded and run out before we fire on them. This is why we're going in at an angle toward their forequarter—to take down sails on their for'ard mast. That mess should slow them down while blinding the gunners below and with some luck fouling their fore chasers as well. Meanwhile we snug in close without taking a hit in the beakhead or across our own foredeck. I trust your mates will get some chain or bar shot loaded and make sure those guns have the elevation. They have to work quickly Paddy. We'll be awfully close by, but this is our one good chance at a first crippling blow before we board. We need those two shots dead-reckoned and then off as soon as the turn is completed and we're within range. We'll get no better opportunity."

"Aye mum—I'll set the guns meself!" he said with a large, admiring, crooked tooth grin before racing forward to help load the two front chasers. She scrambled down to the weather deck to speak to Jengo.

"Keep these boarders ready by, make sure some planks are handy. How we board depends on where any downed mast, rigging, and sails fall." He gave her a gold-toothed smirk and rubbed his hands together but Jez was already meeting with the breathless lad who had delivered her previous orders to helm and quartermaster on the forecastle ladder. With a couple pithy sentences, she sent him running off again to go find their boatswain—Archie was currently the small arms master. As the barefooted youngster sprinted away again, Jez rejoined the boarders.

"You gonna run his legs off!" Jengo said with a forced laugh, and she gave him a quick though grim smile.

"Aye but he's a nimble lad. I told him to let Archie know his lads are to shoot anyone manning a starboard rail gun aboard that galleon and fire on any porthole that starts to open. We're depending on our men with muskets to keep them too busy dodging to be able to target us."

"Sure hope that works," he called after her in a dubious tone as she hastened forward once more to monitor their approach. Jengo had lived through more run-ins with the Spanish coastal patrol than Jez had and he knew they usually kept an ample amount of armed men aboard.

Jez ignored the warning tone in Jengo's voice for she was eager for this threat to be neutralized. They needed to get her own men swarming onto the enemy decks to quell all thoughts of fighting back from those aboard the small Spanish galleon. Their captain did not appear to be all that experienced, or he would have made sure his ship was not so overloaded that he couldn't use his aft guns or turn fast enough to bring to bear whatever firepower he had available. Thankfully *Revelation* was nigh empty of all but the usual supplies for such a short run up the coast. With little livestock and no extra barrels of things necessary for a longer trip, her own good little ship had the speed and the balance for a fast, tight, and rather abrupt change of tack. They should swiftly be within range to fire on the Spaniards.

Yet those aboard the Spanish ship would also be close enough and intensely alert for her attack, though they seemed to have no cannon handy to bring to bear. Every man on that galleon knew that now he would be fighting pirates swarming aboard; it was that or be shamed as cowards. Timing and accuracy were going to mean everything.

While it was still rather too dark to aim well, just before they came into range, gunfire erupted from both of *Revelation*'s two foreward-most rail guns along with some from several men with muskets and one with an old arquebus in the fighting tops directly behind Jez. They couldn't hit much at the oblique angle they were approaching from, but the idea was to keep the galleon's men off-balance. The little brig-rigged pinnace's rail guns were aimed at the foredeck of the larger ship because they weren't in an ideal position to threaten anyone in the tops. They were mostly holding off those on the galleon's own rail guns and while far from accurate, the grapeshot they spewed forced men lining the Spanish ship's starboard side to duck and cover, though there were a few yelps and one protracted scream from a man who was hit while trying to dodge out of the way. He upended over the rail and fell overboard.

That's when some unexpected resistance from the galleon began...

As *Revelation* drew nearly close enough to fire her twin bow chasers, answering salvos came from the tops of the galleon's fore and mainmast where they had both a better standpoint and many more experienced men handling their weapons. Numerous Spanish Marines aboard opened fire again from multiple directions overhead. Most of it was inaccurate but with the varying angles it made enough of a barrage to keep the pirate vessel's fore gunners crouched down. These men were well-trained and steady under fire, though a few had to duck as a couple of well-placed shots hit the wood around them, throwing big splinters that could take out an eye. The sheer amount of gunfire raining down at *Revelation*'s foredeck also allowed the galleon's rail guns to open up. Men on board Jez's ship were scrambling to get out of the way. A couple potential boarders went down as did one of the young powder monkeys. The men were injured mostly by splinters, the boy lay bleeding out from a gut shot, twitching and crying out in agony for his mother. Jengo said some soothing words as he scrambled forward to pick up the dying youngster, carrying him away to hand off to another man.

Paddy took over from the man adjusting the larboard fore cannon when that gunner got winged in the shoulder and was bleeding heavily. "Go wrap it laddie, I got this'n," he said and cranked the aim up for the dead-on shot they needed to end that musket barrage. The doughty little Irish rebel held his position through numerous close shots that sprayed him with fragments of wood until someone got in a lucky hit that ricocheted off the cannon to his right with a bonging noise and hit the back of his head. Still, he managed to fire off his carefully aimed cannon before he collapsed like a felled tree and lay silent as death, blood flowing across the decking in a thin stream. His aim was true though and the whirling bar shot hit about two thirds up the galleon's foremast, which began to topple over as it lost most of its top with sails and rigging collapsing and screaming men tumbling down. The other gunner, a grizzled old veteran, took out enough of the bowsprit to collapse it, throwing sails down over the fore cannon and men in that fighting top into the water. Since they wore partial armor, they sank like rocks. That stopped a good portion of the musket fusillade *Revelation* had been under, for the Spanish marines had been clustered mostly in the two foremost fighting tops.

Jez ordered two other men to carry an unconscious Paddy own below, leaving a thin trail of blood on the deck. Jengo had returned to her side, now that the barrage was over with.

"Quite a few men injured, one may lose his leg. The boy died," he added "Not even time for laudanum to ease his pain."

"Damn it!" she replied through gritted teeth. She turned a quick beseeching look on him. "How in hell were they getting us from that distance?" she asked him as *Revelation* crossed bows with the galleon and the boarders rallied and began to surge to the rail with grapples to throw and make fast before laying planks to make the crossing.

"They always have plenty men with muskets aboard to shoot down at us, the distance be longer that way, but more likely to hit something or someone," he said, his face grim. "Just a few lucky shots adds up."

"I intend to repay them in full for that," she replied as they crossed a plank. She didn't enjoy being made a fool of with their false white flag of surrender. "We'll take everything we can get from these sons of whores and then sink their blasted ship with them all aboard."

It was very uncharacteristic of her to make that call but Jezebel Johnston had had enough of being evenhanded with her enemies. The Spanish had often caused Tortuga a lot of grief. She was going to pay some of that back from now on.

"No quarter," she told her men in a cold-blooded voice with a merciless sneer as they stepped onto the galleon's deck. "Kill anyone who so much as raises a fist."

The End

ABOUT OUR CREATORS

WRITER –

NANCY HANSEN - An avid reader and prolific writer of fantasy and action/adventure fiction for over 30 years, Nancy A. Hansen is the author of many novels, anthologies, and short stories. You can find some of her work at **Pro Se Press** where she has a selection of original offerings of novel length under her imprint *HANSEN'S WAY*, as well as numerous short stories that have been contributed to various Pro Se multi-author publications. She also shares a children's adventure series called *Companion Dragons Tales* with co-authors Roger Stegman and Lee Houston Jr.

At **Airship 27**, Nancy has contributed short stories to *Sinbad-The New Voyages* and *Tales From The Hanging Monkey* anthologies, and she has an ongoing series of the very popular *Jezebel Johnston* pirate novels, including a 4 book omnibus. She also contributed to the Airship 27 anthology, *Legends of New Pulp Fiction* and is a featured author/editor in *Who's Who In New Pulp*. In 2022 she was awarded PULP GRAND MASTER by the members of the Pulp Factory.

Nancy has also written two stories for **Mechanoid Press** in their *Monster Earth* anthologies, and at **Flinch Books** contributed to *Restless: An Anthology of Mummy Horror*. Nancy has a story in the charity anthology *Lost Children*, which benefits groups that help abused and exploited youngsters. Her work on FIRE OF THE BLACK ROSE is her first full-length western novel for **Wolfpack Publishing**. Her initial Chandra Smoake, Paranormal Investigator tale SMOAKE & MIRRORS appeared in *Occult Detective Magazine #7—Spring 2020*.

Nancy has an Amazon Author Page at https://www.amazon.com/Nancy-Hansen/e/B009OGK632/ref=dp_byline_cont_ebooks_3   Her books are also available on Barnes & Noble online and some on Smashwords. She has a writing blog at http://nancyahansen.blogspot.com/ and can also be found on Facebook and Twitter.

Nancy currently resides on an old farm in beautiful, rural eastern Connecticut with an eclectic cast of family members, and one very spoiled dog.

INTERIOR ILLUSTRATIONS –

ROB DAVIS - is an award-winning artist with a 38-plus-year comic book and illustration career. With comics from Marvel, DC, Malibu, Innovation, Caliber and others Rob has worked on series depicting the crews of *Star Trek*'s original series, *the Next Generation*, and *Deep Space Nine*, and other TV series such as *Quantum Leap* and *Pirates of Dark Water*. Characters like Merlin, Robin Hood, Zorro, and Sherlock Holmes have all been subjects of Rob's work. He is presently the Art Director, Designer, and Illustrator for Pulp Revival publisher Airship 27 Productions. He also self-publishes some of his most recent comic book work via his Redbud Studio imprint and is a contributor to Silverline Comics. He is retired from "real work" and lives in central Missouri with his wife, two children, and grandchildren.

COVER ILLUSTRATION–

MICHAEL YOUNGBLOOD —Of Asheville N.C. has a bachelor's degree in art and has done most of his work in architectural illustration and design. He's also done various other freelance projects since 1991.

www.ingramcontent.com/pod-product-compliance
Lightning Source LLC
Chambersburg PA
CBHW070824250626
47170CB00006B/2200